"E[...]
yet heart-tugging romance with the excitement
and drama of the NASCAR world."
—*RT Book Reviews*

"Jean Brashear is an incredibly talented writer."
—*New York Times* bestselling author Stella Cameron

"Jean Brashear's distinctive storytelling voice
instantly draws in the reader."
—#1 *New York Times* bestselling author
Debbie Macomber

"Once again Brashear proves herself
to be an author of fabulous richness,
making her a favorite of romance readers."
—*Midwest Book Reviews*

Praise for Peggy Webb

"Elvis fans are in for a treat…
[with] this comic crime caper."
—*Publishers Weekly* on *Elvis and the Grateful Dead*

"An excellent voice, Southern style and humor
make *Late Bloomers* by Peggy Webb a joy to read…
Wonderful characters, story and heart
make this a winner."
—*RT Book Reviews*

"Laughter through tears is the Southern way,
and…Webb proves it in spades in her latest novel,
Driving Me Crazy."
—*Starkville Daily News*

JEAN BRASHEAR

is a three-time RITA® Award finalist, an *RT Book Reviews* Series Storyteller of the Year and recipient of numerous other awards and has always enjoyed the chance to learn something new while doing research for her books. But never has any subject swept her off her feet like NASCAR. Starting out as someone who wondered what could possibly be interesting about cars driving around a track, she's become a diehard fan, who is only too happy to tell anyone she meets how fascinating the world of NASCAR is. (For pictures of her racing adventures, visit www.jeanbrashear.com.)

PEGGY WEBB

is the bestselling author of more than sixty novels. Her many writing honors include a 2009 Pioneer Award from *RT Book Reviews*. In addition to writing in multiple genres—romance, mystery and women's fiction—this former adjunct instructor at Mississippi State University also writes screenplays. In 2009 Peggy formed an independent film company with documentary filmmaker Roy Turner and actress Philece Sampler. Their first project will be a feature film of Peggy's popular Harlequin NEXT novel, *Driving Me Crazy*. Peggy sings, plays a mean blues piano and has acted in local community theater productions. She also loves gardening and sitting on her front porch with family and friends. She invites you to visit her at www.peggywebb.com.

NASCAR®

Hard to Resist

Jean Brashear & Peggy Webb

HARLEQUIN®

TORONTO • NEW YORK • LONDON
AMSTERDAM • PARIS • SYDNEY • HAMBURG
STOCKHOLM • ATHENS • TOKYO • MILAN • MADRID
PRAGUE • WARSAW • BUDAPEST • AUCKLAND

ISBN-13: 978-0-373-18539-9

HARD TO RESIST

Copyright © 2010 by Harlequin Books S.A.

The publisher acknowledges the
copyright holders of the individual works
as follows:

DOWNRIGHT DISTRACTING
Copyright © 2010 by Harlequin Books S.A.
Jean Brashear is acknowledged as the author of
"Downright Distracting."

SHIFTING GEARS
Copyright © 2010 by Harlequin Books S.A.
Peggy Webb is acknowledged as the author of "Shifting Gears."

Recycling programs
for this product may
not exist in your area.

NASCAR® and the NASCAR Library Collection® are registered
trademarks of the National Association for Stock Car Auto Racing, Inc.

This edition published by arrangement with Harlequin Books S.A.

For questions and comments about the quality of this book
please contact us at Customer_eCare@Harlequin.ca

www.eHarlequin.com

Printed in U.S.A.

CONTENTS

An excerpt from Hilton Branch's prison journal…

Dear God…I thought I was done with them. The courts said there was no money left. Hell, the newspapers, the TV, the Internet—headlines screamed it everywhere. But those thugs at Biscayne Bay don't believe it. Word is somebody new is in charge—Kell Saunders. I seem to remember him. Sat back in the meetings, didn't say much.

But those eyes. Reptile eyes.

He's threatening my children. All of them.

Heaven help me, he knows about Rose. Baby Lily—though she's not a baby now, is she? Two, nearly three, she'd be, and pretty as a picture just like her mama.

I was at my job in the bakery this morning, just another day in an endless stream of them. I'd had a bellyful of being surrounded by thugs—stupid criminals, most of them losers who deserve to be in here—and I was thinking about how some days I want to climb right out of my skin, just haul off and clock somebody, never mind that I've had a heart attack and I'm older than most and not in the best shape. I'd just picked up one tray of bread loaves to stick them in the slicer, when I spotted a piece of paper.

I was about to complain—when I saw my name on it. B-R-A-N-C-H cut out of newspaper print just like in some B-grade movie.

I know things get passed along in mysterious ways around here. The prison grapevine can smuggle not just notes but drugs, money, weapons…there's a crime syndicate in here to equal anything outside, and I've done my best to stay as far away as possible because I want out of here so bad some days I think I'll lose my mind.

I have learned more than I ever wanted to about how careful you have to be. I'd rather live in the sorriest ghetto in the outside world than be in here, where a wrong look, a perceived insult you never meant…the smallest thing can get you killed.

So I've kept my head down, and I've swallowed my pride so often it's just about washed completely away.

The note put all that to waste. Its message was clear as a bell. I am not invisible, there are people watching me.

Biscayne Bay. Kell Saunders.

He wants to know where the money is. He got Fred Clifton— *questioned* him, like this is some movie about drug dealers or terrorists. Fred was my friend once. He hid the money I put aside for Rose and the girls.

Now he's dead.

I have to get word to Rose, but there's no easy way without tipping my hand. There are eyes and ears everywhere. Saunders may not know where she lives—and thank God I never told Fred where to find her—but having Saunders know that she exists, that she's important to me, is danger enough. He won't give up until he hunts her down, her and her daughters.

All I can think to do is string Saunders along and buy time. I cannot let him hurt my Rose, my Lily, my Amelia. Not my grown children, either—I have to warn them…but how, when they want nothing to do with me?

They will hate me more when they know.

But I have to find a way to protect my children.

All of them.

Downright Distracting

Jean Brashear

To all the wonderful authors in the NASCAR series,
thanks for the fun of working together!

And to Ercel, who's taken the ride with me
on more than one harebrained scheme.

CHAPTER ONE

CAN I REALLY BE considering this? Hailey Rogers asked herself.

"Shavasana," she said aloud. Her yoga class complied, assuming the final pose, knowing she would lead them serenely into a relaxation routine that would put the finishing touches on their very strenuous workout. The cherry on top of the sundae…if Hailey still ate sundaes, that is. Or cherries that weren't organically grown.

Hailey herself didn't feel all that relaxed just now. *Empty your mind,* she counseled. Usually becoming one with the flow was as natural as breathing. Today, however, doing so required effort.

But she managed, as she'd had to for years as she sought to make a peaceful existence for herself after growing up with a perpetually dissatisfied mother and minus the father she hadn't seen since she was thirteen.

Yoga and the meditative life were not only a cure but her salvation, her reason for being. That's why this group of rich women had signed on for a very expensive retreat weekend in Santa Fe—because Hailey believed in what she taught and lived it every single day.

So why was she going to risk rocking the boat by contacting her long-absent father? She didn't really have an answer for that, except that in an existence built around peace and well-being, Dixon Rogers was the stone in her sandal, the gnawing mystery of her life.

It's only a phone call. And you need to know. Her relationships with men had been few and fragile because she didn't understand why her father had dropped out of her life. The man she'd been dating most recently wanted more from her than she was willing to give and had leveled some devastating accusations about her caution. She was wary, yes, but also tired of feeling that way, and she'd realized that to move forward, she had to give the male sex a chance by finding out, for once and for all.

Why, Daddy? Why was it so easy to forget me?

As the last of the students departed, Hailey strode with purpose and picked up the cell phone where she'd programmed in a number she'd looked at a thousand times but never used. Before she could wimp out, she scrolled through and punched the call button.

"Fulcrum Racing, how may I help you?"

She'd sort of expected a voice mail system, not an actual person. Hailey swallowed hard before responding. "May I speak with Dixon Rogers, please?"

"Who may I say is calling?"

Hailey gripped the phone hard. "His daughter."

"His daughter?" The soft, Southern voice hesitated. "But Mr. Dixon doesn't—" A male voice in the background spoke swiftly. The woman cleared her throat. "Ah, one moment please."

He's never even told anyone I exist. Hailey nearly hung up then, but before she could, a man's voice came on the line.

"Hailey? Is it really you, sweetheart?"

Even though she hadn't heard him speak in fourteen years, that voice rose from long-buried memory. Tears crowded her throat.

Sweetheart. He called me sweetheart. Not in a million years had she expected that.

So exactly where have you been all my life, Daddy?

"HEY, RYDER, THEY HUNG the car body for Bristol, but I don't know, man..."

Crew chief Ryder McGraw looked up from the spreadsheet

he was building, switching gears instantly as he had to do many times a day. "What's wrong with it?"

His car chief, Marcus Conroy, responsible for setting up all the cars for the No. 464 team of Fulcrum Racing, shook his head. "I don't think that tweak to the front bumper is going to make tech inspection, not the way it's fabricated right now."

Ryder didn't react with the frustration he felt. Every microscopic facet of the race operation was ultimately his responsibility, including personality conflicts between the shop's fabricators and his increasingly difficult car chief. "You think…or you *know,* Marcus?"

The clench in Marcus's jaw didn't bode well. Marcus had wanted Ryder's job, but he'd never get it, not when he was becoming less and less a team player by the day.

Ryder opened his mouth to respond just as one of the engineers appeared in his office doorway with a shock absorber in his hand.

"Bingo. Ryder—I'm officially a genius! This baby's gonna make Jeb Stallworth the best road course driver anyone's ever seen. Oh—" The engineer faltered as he spotted Marcus in front of him.

Ryder held up a hand. "Hang on, don't go anywhere. I want to see this." He turned to the car chief. "Marcus, get me tolerances on the new body and shoot them to me ASAP. I'll come look as soon as I can."

"But, Ryder—"

Ryder's phone rang. "Hold on. McGraw," he answered.

"I need you in my office right now." Dixon Rogers, the team owner. His voice was strained. He probably wanted to discuss Jeb's less-than-stellar race at Indy.

"Will do." Ryder clicked off. The pressures of forming a brand-new team would have him eating aspirin like candy if he allowed himself.

But he loved racing. And he owed Dixon Rogers everything.

Including a championship-caliber team.

Which he would deliver if it killed him.

Marcus was still lurking. The engineer stood in the doorway.

"I said I'd be there, Marcus, as soon as you get me the data." He turned to the engineer. "I have to head for Dixon's office. Walk with me." He moved into the hallway, stopped every second or two to sign something or make a decision or give advice. To each person he tried to give his full attention because team cohesion was critical. Each member was important, and he wanted them to feel that way.

It was only ten-thirty in the morning. He'd been here since five and would be lucky to leave by midnight, but he held out a hand for the shock, smiling. "Let me see that beauty." He studied it as he walked and whistled appreciation. "Get me that win at Watkins Glen and I'll name my firstborn after you."

The engineer chuckled. "Since you never take time to date, I'm not holding my breath."

Ryder couldn't argue. Personal time was way down low on his agenda. "Well...someday." He returned the equipment and paused at Dixon Rogers's door. "Looks good. Let's get one into a practice car and see how it tests." He clapped the man on the shoulder, then started to knock just as the door was yanked open.

Dixon Rogers stood on the other side of the doorway, a strange expression on his face. "Come in, come in." He closed the door behind Ryder. "How are you today, Ryder?"

"Fine, sir." Ryder resisted the urge to frown. "You doing okay?" Dixon's color was high, and there was a slightly manic air about him, unusual for a generally calm man.

"Couldn't be better," he said. "Have a seat." He gestured toward the chair in front of his desk.

"About last week—"

"I'm not concerned about Indy."

Ryder did frown then. Finishing thirty-fourth was hardly a

matter to blow off. "Why not? It was inexcusable. Set us back in points."

It was Dixon's turn to furrow his forehead. "I know. But I have faith in you. There's not a better crew chief in the garage."

Ryder wished he shared the optimism. He was good, he knew that, but he was only one piece, and a championship team required all the members to perform flawlessly. He still had weak points, such as Marcus. "Mr. Rogers…" he began.

"How many times have I told you to call me Dixon? You're not a wet-behind-the-ears mechanic anymore." Dixon chuckled. "I swear I never saw anyone bust their butt like you. Probably never will again."

"I had a lot to prove."

"Not to me. Not for long, anyway."

Ryder loved this man who was like a second father to him. There was nothing he wouldn't do to repay the confidence Dixon had bestowed by bringing him up through the ranks. "Thank you, sir." At Dixon's lifted brow, he amended, "Dixon. Just feels weird."

After a pause, Ryder continued with his original point. "I think I'm going to have to replace Marcus, maybe before the season's over."

At the same moment, Dixon spoke. "I have a favor to ask. I need your help."

"What did you say?" both responded.

"You first," Ryder said.

"You want to replace Marcus?"

Ryder prepared for an argument, though Dixon mostly left decisions in his hands—with the exception that his boss was tight with money. But as long as Ryder kept expenses in line, he was okay. "His ego's getting in the way. We can't have that. Most of the good car chiefs are working, but I was thinking about Bodie Martin."

Dixon's eyebrows lifted. "He's been out of the game awhile."

"Yes, but when he was in, there was no one better." Ryder cocked his head. "Think I'm crazy for going with an old-school guy?"

Dixon shook his head slowly, grin widening. "Nope, I'm thinking you just might be a genius, son. There's something to be said for age and experience." But even as he spoke, worry slid over his features and he stared off into the distance.

"But what?"

Dixon snapped back to attention. "Nothing. Not to do with Bodie, I mean. You go ahead if you think you want him. I trust you with the budget, as well as the team." Then he rose and started to pace.

"What's wrong, Dixon?"

The older man was staring out his office window, jingling the change in his pockets. "You ever made a bad mistake you'd give anything to fix, Ryder?"

Ryder tried to imagine what he could be referring to. It had to be something to do with the team because in the twelve years he'd been with Dixon Rogers, they had never discussed anything personal. "You haven't made any big mistakes with your racing teams, far as I can tell."

Dixon turned, his gaze piercing. "This isn't about racing. It's what I wanted to talk to you about."

What could have the man so concerned? Ryder waited.

"This is about my daughter."

Ryder's eyes popped. "You have a daughter?" So far as anyone around here knew, Dixon's life began and ended at the track.

"Hailey. She's twenty-six—no, twenty-seven, I think. I haven't seen her since not long after her mother and I divorced. She was just turning thirteen." His expression was filled with regret.

Ryder wondered what had happened, but he had never been one to meddle, so he remained silent.

"She called me today." If Ryder hadn't known better, he'd have thought the older man had tears in his eyes. "I didn't

even know where she was, though I've wished I did." He
glanced away and swiped at his eyes with finger and thumb.
"I want her back in my life, Ryder. I loved that little girl with
everything in me."

Yet you haven't seen her in this long? Ryder bit back the
question. Again…none of his business.

"And that's where you come in."

"Me?"

"I've invited her to spend the next month with us, here at
the shop and traveling with the team. I want you to help me
make her feel comfortable."

I'm not a social director, Ryder wanted to say. *I'm trying
to build a championship team, and I don't have time to squire
some princess around.*

But he said none of that. Everything he had he owed to
Dixon Rogers, and he was genuinely fond of the man, as well.
"What does she do for a living? She can take this much time
off, a whole month?" *No. Please say no.*

Dixon's face creased in a grin. "Well, that's interesting,
actually." If anything his smile grew wider. "She's a yoga
instructor, apparently."

Ryder blinked. "Yoga?"

Dixon shrugged. "She grew up in California. What can I
say?"

Oh, great. Just great. Estranged daughter from la-la land,
a freakin' yoga instructor. Could this day get any better?

"I think I'm speechless." He rose.

Dixon had the sense of humor to chuckle. "I hear you. Her
mother was not a fan of racing, you know." Yet he was filled
with cheer. "I'm counting on you to help me show her how
great my world is. I want her free to roam anywhere in the
operation and make herself right at home."

Ryder opened his mouth then immediately shut it. Aside
from safety issues—which were considerable—the likelihood
that this flake from the Left Coast would find any of Fulcrum
remotely interesting didn't seem high to him.

But that would be to the good. Maybe she could just go twist herself into a pretzel or whatever in a vacant corner or the conference room or…somewhere. Anywhere he didn't have to add her to the list of his daily duties, one that seemed endless already.

"How soon will she arrive?"

"She's finishing up at some fancy resort in Santa Fe today. I'm sending the plane for her in the morning."

Holy crap. Dixon was serious. He wouldn't send a whole plane for one person unless that person was important…really important. Well, surely she'd want to rest up, get acquainted with her dad the first few days, so maybe he'd be free of her until after Pocono, if he were lucky. "I'll look forward to meeting her. Now I'd better go see what Marcus is carping about on the new body for Bristol."

Dixon clapped him on the shoulder and squeezed. "I appreciate this, Ryder. It means a lot to me for her to like this place and what I do. She's my only child."

The vulnerability in the older man's eyes got to Ryder more than he wanted it to. He wasn't used to Dixon being emotional about anything. "I'll do my best, sir."

"I know you will. You always do, and I'm grateful."

But not grateful enough to give this duty to Hugo Murphy, Fulcrum's other crew chief. Though the very thought made Ryder grin. Hugo was an excellent crew chief and actually a good guy, but he was crusty as hell and would likely scare Dixon's cupcake of a daughter right out of town before she ever got past Hugo's bluster.

Ryder was pondering what on earth he would do to entertain a yoga instructor in the land of gearheads, when one of the mechanics came charging down the hall toward him. "Ryder, the cylinder honing machine just broke, right in the middle of getting next week's engine ready."

The last thing they had the budget for was replacing an expensive piece of equipment, but this one was crucial. "How bad?"

Words tumbled in a rush as they picked up their pace down the hall.

I'll think about the cupcake tomorrow, Ryder decided. *I'm all out of time now.*

CHAPTER TWO

HAILEY STILL COULDN'T believe she'd been flown to Charlotte on a private jet. She dealt with wealthy people often, yes, but she herself lived quite modestly, and she preferred things that way. Her mother had constantly criticized her father for spending money on race cars instead of on them, but from what Hailey could tell, her dad had sent child support like clockwork. He'd also sent birthday and Christmas gifts, even if they'd often been out of touch with her age or interests.

What he had failed to do was be present or even to call.

But that's the past, she reminded herself. This is about the present moment. "Be here now" was her mantra. Despite her nerves over seeing her father again, she was resolute about maintaining that attitude.

When she stepped off the plane, the humidity slapped her first, followed by the heat. "Wow."

The pilot smiled. "Welcome to the South, Ms. Rogers."

"Thank you. I think."

He grinned. "Takes some getting used to. I'll get your bag. You go on ahead. Ryder's waiting just over there."

"Ryder?"

"He's one of your dad's crew chiefs. I'm actually surprised he's here. He's a really busy man."

And why isn't my father here if he's so eager to see me?

Deep breath. *Be here now.* "Then I'd better hurry up, I suppose." She took her bag from the pilot and started across the tarmac toward the tall, dark-haired man telegraphing his impatience over the yards between them.

WHOA, RYDER WAS thinking. *She's a looker.* Slim and grace-ful, with legs a mile long and white-blond hair in a braid that reached her hips, Hailey Rogers had inherited none of her features from her father, that much he could tell. Damn. He hadn't been prepared for her to be gorgeous.

Her steps slowed as she approached, and he remembered his manners at last. "Ms. Rogers, I'm Ryder McGraw. Your dad couldn't be here, though he wanted to. We had a sponsor drop in unannounced, and especially in this economy, you don't leave a sponsor hanging. He's sure sorry, though."

"Is he?" Pale blue eyes revealed her skepticism.

He reached for her bag. "I swear it. Your visit is important to him. He's a good man."

"I wouldn't know." She averted her face and fell into step with him.

Miss Iceberg, not a cupcake, apparently. "He's nervous about seeing you." Then Ryder wanted to kick himself. What the devil was he thinking, revealing Dixon's vulnerability to the princess?

But Miss Iceberg glanced at him, and ice wasn't what he saw at all. More like—oh, hell, was she going to cry?

Why had he agreed to come get her, no matter how much he owed Dixon? His lists had lists, and he had to fly out to Pocono tomorrow.

"Look, Ms. Rogers…" But even as he was speaking, she was straightening her shoulders, and the bad moment had passed.

"So what does a crew chief do?" she asked.

Ryder breathed a sigh of relief that he wouldn't have to console her after all, and he began to explain.

HAILEY TRIED TO LISTEN as Ryder McGraw went through a dizzying litany of terms she would never in a million years remember, but all she could think was that this was a mistake.

She should never have come. And staying a whole month was clearly impossible.

"—other questions?"

She blinked. "Pardon me?"

He speared her with those unbelievably green eyes—mossy green, Pacific Northwest forest-green—and she had to work very hard to hear his words. "Do you have any other questions?"

"No—no, thank you." But then she glanced around her. "On second thought, is there an organic grocery in town? Or a farmers' market?"

"I have no idea." He glanced over at her. "So you really are from California, aren't you?"

"What's that supposed to mean?"

Broad shoulders shrugged. "Nothing, only…uh, I'm guessing that barbecue for lunch wouldn't be a good idea?"

She gasped and slapped one hand to her chest before she saw the challenge in his eyes. "I haven't eaten meat since I graduated from high school, if that's what you're asking."

He nodded. "Yep." Then he chuckled.

"What?"

"Nothing." But his brow furrowed. "I'm supposed to take you to lunch while Dixon wines and dines the sponsor. I'm trying to figure if Sheila could scare up something for a vegetarian or vegan or whatever you are. She serves one hell of a meat loaf over at Maudie's Down Home Diner, and her baby back ribs are impressive, too."

Hailey resisted a shudder. "I have granola in my bag. I'll be fine."

"No one can survive on granola, Ms. Rogers."

"Hailey," she corrected. "And you've never eaten my granola."

Dark brows winged upward. "You make your own?"

"I do. Commercial varieties are loaded with sugar and preservatives."

He really did have the most beautiful smile—if only his amusement wasn't directed at her. "And we wouldn't want that, right?"

"What you put in your body and how you care for it determines the quality of your life."

"My body feels pretty happy after a good sausage-and-rib dinner—with a side of potato salad, maybe some banana pudding for dessert."

She had a sense that partly he was simply fencing with her, but there was a definite element of seriousness, too. "You have no idea what you're doing to yourself or how much better you could feel."

"I'm a busy man, Ms. Rogers." Pointedly he ignored her request to use her given name. "I don't have time for touchy-feely foolishness. We're here," he continued before she could argue. "I guess granola it is."

She emerged from the company car and grabbed her suitcase before he could. "Thank you for the ride," she said in a prim tone she hardly recognized.

Then she strode ahead of him into the side door emblazoned with Fulcrum Racing's logo.

Breathe. You can leave anytime you want. Just...breathe.

A curvy brunette approached. "Sue Ellen, this is Dixon's daughter," he said. "If you'd make her at home, I'd appreciate it."

Sue Ellen flashed a smile that revealed dimples. "Sure thing, Ryder." She grabbed a stack of message slips. "Here are the calls you missed."

"Thanks," he said with a sigh. He turned to Hailey. "Welcome to NASCAR, Ms. Rogers." He tipped an imaginary hat and strode off.

"Is that man gorgeous or what?" the receptionist said. "Too bad all he ever does is work."

Hailey forced a smile. *Maybe you could cook him a...a*

hog or something and cheer him up. But instead, she simply asked, "Is there somewhere I could freshen up?"

"Oh, absolutely, sugar. Follow me!"

WHEN SHE EMERGED, Hailey was smoothing on an aromatherapy lotion named Calm Breezes. She headed back in the direction she recalled, spotting racing photos along the wall. She stopped before one of them and saw her father standing with a man in some kind of racing suit, trophy held high between them. Her father looked so happy.

She tried to imagine herself there beside him. All her life she'd heard about how rough racing people were, about the noise and the fumes, but never once had her mother focused on this part—how jubilant everyone was, the twenty or thirty people lined up behind the driver and her father, cheering.

"Sweetheart. Hailey."

She jolted and turned.

And there he was, an older version she hardly recognized. The man she remembered had sandy hair, not gray, and he'd been lean and energetic. This man's shoulders were more rounded, his posture less straight, his jaw not so firm.

But the blue eyes she'd inherited from him were smiling the way she'd have given anything to see them so many, many days and nights of her childhood.

"Daddy—" She started forward but brought herself up short when she realized someone was with him. "Oh, I'm sorry."

"Brandon Granger," her father said, "this is my daughter, Hailey. Hailey, Brandon is the president of Secure Communications, sponsor of Jeb Stallworth's car. You met Ryder, right?"

She nodded and held out a hand. "Pleased to meet you."

Brandon Granger, much younger—better looking, too, in a preppy sort of way—than she'd expected when she'd heard her father was entertaining a sponsor, shook hers with a firm grip. "Your father tells me you're from California."

"Originally. I've been teaching in Santa Fe a lot over the last year."

"Love Santa Fe. The people, the culture. The food." He rolled his eyes in an expression of bliss. "I envy you the time there."

"It's amazing, all right."

"Maybe we should get together while you're here, compare notes." A decidedly interested gleam lit his gaze.

I don't think I'll be here long, she would have said a few minutes earlier, but this man was evidence that the South wasn't filled with Neanderthals like Ryder McGraw.

She cast a quick glance at her father to see if this would be a problem. He only smiled proudly and nodded. "I'd enjoy that," she responded.

Finally, Brandon let go of her hand. "Well, I understand you two haven't seen each other in a while, so I'll run along. Dixon, you've got one fine crew chief in Ryder. I'm feeling good about the next few years."

"Ryder has the brightest future in NASCAR. Jeb's delighted to be working with him," her father responded.

"See you on Saturday, then."

"You're coming to the race, after all?"

The sponsor cast a quick glance at Hailey, then back. "I'll make time."

Her father's face was wreathed in a pleased smile. "See you this weekend."

Brandon Granger departed, leaving Hailey and her father standing a mere two feet apart, but suddenly the distance felt like miles and just as awkward.

"He seems nice," she said to fill the silence.

"Hailey—" Her father halted.

She looked at him then, shocked to see his eyes suspiciously bright. "Yes?"

He opened his arms. "I am so sorry, sweetheart. I thought I was doing the right thing, letting you get on with your life, but I missed you so much. Can you ever forgive me?"

When she hesitated, his arms started to lower.

"Oh, Daddy, I missed you, too," Hailey said.

And moved into the embrace she'd waited half a life-time for.

CHAPTER THREE

RYDER, WHY DON'T YOU join us? Dixon had asked the question the day before, as he was showing Hailey around the shop.

If Ryder hadn't seen the nerves in his boss's eyes, he would have tried harder to get out of the tour. He didn't have time, but Dixon knew that, so he must have really felt the need for Ryder's presence.

The tour had been almost comical. Granola Girl was trying, he had to admit, but if she'd been dumped out of a plane onto the surface of Mars, she couldn't have been farther outside her comfort zone. She didn't hear the sweet music of a well-tuned engine, instead, she wanted to know if they'd read any studies on the effects of noise on human hearing.

Like he wasn't a stickler for ear protection, in the shop or at the track.

She studied the pit crew and interrogated their trainer about stretching techniques, then started grilling them on their diets.

As if he weren't concerned about their health already. A team could only perform as well as its pit crew did.

When Dixon had said he'd take her to breakfast at Maudie's—which every race shop in Mooresville knew was the best breakfast in America—she'd wrinkled her nose, glanced over at Ryder and offered to cook for Dixon instead.

Ryder shuddered. God knows what his boss had been forced to eat this morning. Scrambled tofu with alfalfa? Wheat straw with ground acorns or some other such torture?

He'd had a fine breakfast at Maudie's himself—eggs, ham,

grits and biscuits fit to die for. That Sheila Trueblood's cook Al had a real knack in the kitchen.

An undertow of laughter in the shop dragged Ryder from his laptop screen. He glanced out the window of his office to the shop floor to see his men huddled in animated conversation and then, one by one, they headed for the back of the shop to peer out of a cracked-open back door.

All work had stopped. He rose to see what was going on. As he approached, the group scattered.

"What's up?" he asked.

Merriment danced in the eyes of Ray Levinson, one of Fulcrum's engine specialists. "Words don't do it justice. You'd better look for yourself."

Ryder's brow furrowed, but he followed Ray over to the back door.

"Damn, but that girl's got some legs on her," said one mechanic in tones of reverence.

"Those legs aren't all that could stop a man's heart," said the parts guy who peered over his shoulder.

Ryder had the sinking feeling he didn't need to look to know who they were talking about. "Guys?" he said mildly even as he simmered. "Everyone got their work done?"

The two men jumped as like scalded cats. "Oh, hey, Ryder. We were just—"

"No harm meant, Ryder, it's only—"

They stumbled over each other in their haste to get out of his way.

He simply stood there with one eyebrow arched, arms folded across his chest.

In a half second, both were gone, yet Ryder didn't move from where he was.

"Wanna look, boss?" asked Ray.

"I really don't think so," he replied. "But I guess I have to."

"Don't blame the boys. Any red-blooded man would have a hard time ignoring a sight like that."

Ryder stepped forward and peered outside.

Then closed his eyes and counted to ten. Opened them again.

She was still there. Hailey, in some tank top and exercise pants that clung to her every curve in a manner guaranteed to make a grown man break into a cold sweat. Yes, the guys were right—her legs were a mile long. Her behind was taut and rounded and pure temptation to a man's hands as she bent over at the waist, feet together and knees locked, damn near laying her elbows on the ground.

What a man could do with a woman that flexible...

But she was doing it in front of his pit crew, and challenging them to follow her lead.

They'd all be crippled by midmorning.

Hell. Ryder slapped the door frame and strode outside, already opening his mouth to bark at her—

When he saw his team owner standing in the shade, a wide grin on his face. As Ryder approached, Dixon spoke. "Isn't she something? I've never seen anything like her."

Count to twenty this time, Ryder lectured himself. "Yeah, amazing," he finally answered. And was, he had to admit, impressed when she moved down to her mat with her legs spread in a wide V, her torso bent forward, flat on the ground. "But the guys are going to wind up with torn muscles and strained ligaments."

"She says they won't. She's only demonstrating right now, but she says she can make them more flexible by at least thirty percent, maybe more, by the time she leaves." Dixon's tone was all admiration and pride. "The guys seem enthusiastic."

The guys are watching the same distraction, likely with the same pure male response the guys inside are...*were*, he corrected, with a snapping glance backward to be sure the door was closed. They'd better be working now.

Not that he could blame them. Granola Girl was some kind of gorgeous.

But she was a problem, nonetheless. One that had to

be handled carefully. "What did you have for breakfast, Dixon?"

The team owner's gaze shifted to him. "An egg white omelet with goat cheese and chives," he said carefully.

Figures, Ryder thought.

"It was surprisingly delicious."

Ryder met Dixon's gaze, trying not to grin. "I bet."

The two men stood silent for a moment, then Ryder stirred. "I'm just going to have a little chat to find out more about her methods, okay?" he said to Dixon.

Dixon nodded. "I have a meeting, anyway. Want to join us for lunch? Hailey says she likes to cook."

Not even if I were starving, Ryder thought. "Thanks. Let me see how the morning goes first. A lot left on my checklist before we leave."

"Sure thing."

Ryder walked away. "Ms. Rogers, may I have a word with you?" he called out.

The pit crew, completely absorbed in Hailey until he'd spoken, jumped as if shot.

"Hey, Ryder."

"Hi, boss."

"Isn't she something?"

"Yeah, something, all right," he agreed, never taking his eyes off her.

Hailey rose in one supple move, stepped into her sandals, then turned to face him. "Mr. McGraw." Her eyes were wide and lively. "How are you?"

"Fine, just fine," he said through clenched jaw, clasping her elbow and leading her off to the side under the shade of the building's overhang. "What the hell are you doing to my crew?" he said quietly.

"Teaching. It's what I do. My father thought it was a good idea. I can help them improve. Their conditioning is too much about power and not enough about flexibility."

Your father has gone soft in the head, he wanted to say.

"Their regimen has been designed by one of the best trainers in the business." Who would be arriving within the hour.

That fat braid shifted over her chest as she sniffed and tossed her head. "I can do better."

Do not stare at her figure. Especially not those blasted mile-long legs. He struggled for patience. "That's a real fine offer, Ms. Rogers, but you're here on vacation. We couldn't possibly presume upon you."

The quirk of her mouth said she knew what he was trying to do. "Oh, I don't mind a bit, Mr. McGraw. I'm happy to help my father's team." Emphasis on *my father's*. As in *not yours, Ryder McGraw.*

But it *was* his team. If she wanted to interfere, let her interfere with Hugo's bunch, but not his. He had enough to handle, trying to give Jeb Stallworth the car and the team and the championship the gifted, long-denied driver deserved.

Then he had an idea. "Tell you what. If Greg Schiffer likes the idea, then fine—but you do things on his schedule, you hear me? The pit crew is too crucial to the team's success, and we can't be having injuries."

She barely resisted rolling her eyes. "I wouldn't be very good at what I do if I let my students get injured. A good yoga instructor is prepared to work with each student at his or her level." She straightened and put her hands on her hips. "And I'm a very good yoga instructor."

"I'm sure you are." *Not.* Okay, maybe she was, but she was also nosy and interfering and in his way. But he summoned a smile he didn't feel. "And for your information, if you can keep from strutting yourself in front of the rest of my men, both your father and I would appreciate it."

"Strutting!" Outrage skated over her features. "I was doing no such thing." Then her forehead wrinkled and she bent closer. "They were watching, really?"

"Babe, they were drooling."

Her brows snapped together. "That's sexist."

"That's men, sugar. Not that the demonstration wasn't

impressive." He leaned in, conscious of a light, flowery scent that was altogether too pleasant. "My guys are only human, and I need them focused. If you're going to flaunt your flexibility, do it somewhere else, but not in my shop. We clear on that?"

Pale blue eyes turned to ice. "Perfectly."

"Greg can arrange for better space that's not out in the heat, for one thing."

"Heat keeps your muscles fluid. I teach a body flow class that would have them all dripping with sweat in the first five minutes."

"No way. My guys are tough and strong."

"Your guys can't keep up with me."

Damned if she didn't fire his blood, those eyes sparking, that slim body rigid with outrage. "I'll leave that to you and Greg. Now, some of us have to work." He strolled off, confident that he'd solved his problem and she'd go fruit shopping or something now. Greg Schiffer was a tyrant. He wouldn't just dislike the idea, he would hate it. Ryder was aware that a team or two had experimented with yoga, but he needed certainty. Fewer variables, not more. Now was not the time to tinker with the team he'd put everything into building.

Twenty-nine days to go. Might as well be a lifetime.

Ryder sighed and kept walking.

SUE ELLEN STOPPED in his doorway. "Boss man wants to know if you're ready to grab a bite with him and Hailey."

Ryder looked up from the engine performance spreadsheet. "Tell him sorry but I'll just order in."

"Want the usual, cheeseburger and fries from Maudie's?" she asked.

"Sounds great. Thanks, Sue Ellen." He returned his attention to the screen, studying something that puzzled him.

"You need to get a life, Ryder. When's the last time you left the shop before midnight? A man can't live on takeout, even Sheila's."

"Thanks, Mom. Go away."

Sue Ellen sighed loudly. "Your mother must be a saint."

"Nope. Five foot three, red hair and the devil's own temper." He loved her to distraction, as did all her kids and her husband of forty years.

"Maybe she could get you to see reason. I should call her."

"Now that's just nasty. I had no idea you had such a mean streak, Sue Ellen." Ryder dragged his gaze away from the screen long enough to grin.

She grinned back. "Don't think I won't, young man."

"I'm shaking. Now go away so I can concentrate."

"I'm going shopping first. Maybe I'll buy shoes. You might not get to eat for two more hours."

Her threats fell on deaf ears. "There's always the vending machines."

"You are hopeless."

"I love you, too."

Both satisfied with the exchange, Sue Ellen left for lunch, and Ryder returned to work.

Some indeterminate time later, a plate was shoved onto the desk beside him. Ryder grunted his thanks, dragged some bills from his pocket and threw them onto the desk to repay Sue Ellen, then returned to his keyboard.

A few seconds later, the scent hit him. Whatever this was, it wasn't French fries. Not a burger. Cautiously he tipped up the cover over the plate.

He scowled. "Is this a joke, Sue Ellen?" he yelled.

"Your health is no joke." The speaker was not Sue Ellen. Hailey Rogers stood before him, no longer attired in her yoga pants but instead in a short pastel blue skirt with a scoop-necked filmy blouse, also blue and dotted with flowers.

"Um...thanks, but I already ordered. My lunch will be here any minute."

"How do you expect your team members to eat healthy if you don't?"

"I'm not their nanny. All I care about is how they do their jobs."

"They'll work better if they take care of themselves." She rattled off enough health statistics and studies to rival any of his engineering staff's geeky lingo. "Try it. It's good. My father loved it."

"Your father ate an egg white omelet. He'd munch on meadow grass to make you happy."

"Chicken."

"I am not."

She smirked. "I mean that's chicken, stir fried with almonds and veggies over brown rice." She paused. "Not that the other doesn't apply, Mr. Picky."

His eyes narrowed. "I'm not a picky eater."

One slim eyebrow arched. "Could have fooled me."

He glanced at the plate. "Chicken? You sure?"

"I don't care for meat myself, but I know how to prepare it for those who are addicted to the taste of flesh."

His head rose as he prepared to glare. Then he spotted a small twinkle in her eyes. "You make meat eaters sound barbaric."

"Only some of them." He could swear her mouth twitched.

"All right, all right." He stabbed with his fork and popped a bite in his mouth, prepared to hate it.

It was actually pretty tasty—for sissy food. Not that he'd tell her.

"So?" She moved closer, and he could smell her again, that light, flowery scent that said pure female.

But he didn't do light and flowery. Though he actually hadn't had a date in long enough that he wasn't sure if he had a type. "It's okay," he grumbled.

For a second, she looked hurt. Then she yanked the plate out from under him and spun, heading for the door on those long, slender, killer legs. Hell, even her feet were sexy, clad in thin-strapped flat sandals with some kind of jewels on them.

"Wait! Where are you going?"

"To feed someone who appreciates the time I put into making the meal."

His mother would take him to the woodshed for treating anyone like this. He rose and intercepted her, snagging the plate and holding it out of her reach. "I didn't say I wouldn't eat it."

"Don't do me any favors, Mr. Grumpy."

He jolted. "Mr. Grumpy?"

She stuck her pretty nose in the air and stabbed a finger into his chest.

For some perverse reason, he wanted to grab that finger and nibble on it. To take that passion and see what he could do to please them both.

Good gravy. Sue Ellen was right. He definitely needed to get out more.

"Well, Brandon loved it, I'll have you know." She slipped around him. "He ate two helpings."

"Brandon?"

"Granger. He asked if I'd teach him how to cook this while we're in Pocono." She turned on her heel and marched out the door, that sassy behind swaying with every step.

"Brandon?" he echoed as if he was half-stupid. He rushed for the door. "Why are you going to Pocono with my sponsor?" he roared.

She merely waved one slim hand over her shoulder and disappeared around the corner.

Ryder stared after her and absently took a bite. *"Brandon,"* he mocked in a singsong tone. "Brandon just loved it, did he?"

When he looked down, he'd cleared half the plate.

CHAPTER FOUR

HAILEY WASN'T SURE what she'd expected from a race week-end, but the reality of it surprised her. The team was busy from dawn until midnight, and the atmosphere was a combination of jaw-clenching tension and an electric excitement. Outside, the fans were jubilant and thrilled to be there—she could see pleasure written all over their faces, sort of like your birthday and Christmas all rolled together.

But inside the garage, she began to understand the stakes. Yes, team members apparently loved racing with every cell in their bodies, but there was a lot on the line every single weekend. Each one of them burned with the fire of competition. For someone who'd devoted her life to peace and serenity, the charged atmosphere was more than a little unsettling.

It was also exciting like nothing she'd ever experienced. She found herself falling under the spell so that by race time, she was at fever pitch herself. The pageantry was stunning, and she found herself regretting having agreed to sit in Brandon's suite instead of down with the team.

Her father had agreed to be upstairs, as well, but she could tell that he was eager to be with his men. "Go on down, Daddy," she urged him. "You don't have to stay with me."

Longing flickered but he shook his head. "I want to watch your first race with you."

Hailey glanced over at Brandon, who was talking to some of his executives, then back to her dad. "Would it cause you problems with your sponsor if we both went downstairs?"

His eyes lit. "I don't care if it does." At her frown, he went on. "But he'll understand. Anyone who loves racing would."

So it was that Hailey found herself down at track level, sitting in the pit box beside Ryder while her father sat in the back. She'd protested that she didn't want to be in the way, but her father was determined that she get the fullest experience and assured her she wouldn't be an intrusion.

Ryder, she was fairly certain, did not agree, but to his credit, he didn't argue. As she listened to him and the driver, Jeb, and spotter, Mike Thompson, though, she was impressed. Ryder was clearly the busiest man on the team and under no small amount of pressure, yet he spoke calmly to everyone and kept his head even when Jeb was nearly wrecked and became very agitated for a while. Ryder never appeared ruffled but got Jeb refocused and seemed to adjust his strategy on the fly.

Not that she understood all this without her father explaining a great deal of what was going on, but what she did understand was that Ryder McGraw was able to keep a cool head under very challenging circumstances.

As could she. She watched the pit crew perform and was sincerely impressed, but she remained convinced that she could help them be even better at their jobs.

Unfortunately, Greg Schiffer hadn't agreed. He'd turned her down flat on her proposal to work with the crew on flexibility.

But Hailey found herself wanting, in her time with the team, to make a contribution. She wasn't a person to sit around idle, nor did she like to shop, though her father had made it clear that he'd love to spend money on her. He didn't owe her anything, though—that wasn't what this visit was about.

Right then, Hailey decided what she would do. Maybe she couldn't actually train the pit crew, but a couple of them had seemed somewhat interested in gaining flexibility and weren't intimidated by the idea of trying yoga. Her father wanted to give her something, so maybe she'd ask for a space to conduct an in-house yoga class, open to whomever might like to try it. And if she wanted to do a little cooking for interested parties, well, there was more than one way to skin a cat, right? Even if she only educated a person or two, that was what she'd devoted her life to and she wouldn't be just hanging around, getting in the way.

She glanced over at the very serious—and seriously sexy, not that she cared—Ryder McGraw and smiled to herself. He was so sure she was full of it, but he was dead wrong. What you put into your body and how you cared for it were essential to your well-being. Youth wouldn't protect you forever.

He was dictatorial and stubborn and had his mind made up. A month—well, three weeks plus now—wasn't enough time to make major changes, but it was long enough for some level of improvement in physical conditioning and renewed energy.

He would have to be convinced, but there was a part of her that liked a challenge. Serenity was wonderful, but maybe she was her father's daughter, after all.

Winning was a matter of definition.

And it was fun.

Just then, the voices in the headset, the zing of adrenaline she felt all around her and a glance at the tower told her that the race was nearing its end and Jeb Stallworth was in the top ten.

Ryder never turned a hair while he spoke as calmly as ever.

But his body was like a live wire fully charged.

The fans were on their feet, the team leaning forward, intent upon the action. Hailey found herself on the edge of her seat, too.

And when the race ended with Jeb in ninth spot, her father roared his approval, and even stuffy old Ryder gave her a high-five.

MONDAYS WERE WHEN the race shop was most quiet. Ryder himself generally came in, as did the guys responsible for building the cars. Still, depending upon how the team had finished in the previous race, the atmosphere could be less pressured.

"You should be in bed asleep," said Sue Ellen when she found him already two hours into work before anyone else arrived.

"Too much to do." He turned back to his laptop.

"Did you even eat breakfast?"

He dropped his head in exasperation. "Sheila made me eggs and bacon first thing. Now will you go away?"

Her eyes sparkled. "You did good this weekend, Ryder. This team is coming along."

"Should have had a top five," he grumbled.

"You're gonna have an ulcer before you turn forty. You ought to get Hailey to teach you yoga. Learn to meditate or something."

All manner of retorts sprang to his lips, but he restrained himself. "Yeah, that's gonna happen. Are you done lecturing me for one morning?"

"I'm just saying." She grinned and walked off.

Three hours later, his stomach growled and Ryder made a split-second decision to go out for lunch for a change. He was nearly to the doors that opened onto the reception and display area when motion in the conference room caught his eye.

The lighting was dimmed, and the conference table shoved to one wall. He didn't need to waste time speculating on how such an unusual situation came to be. All he had to do was look at the woman in front of the far wall.

Hailey stretched her arms high and bent her head back, speaking softly as she moved. Her long blond braid swung level with the tops of her thighs. Then she bent forward at the waist, feet flat on the floor, knees straight, her hands also flat on the floor in front of her.

Ryder caught himself imagining performing that same bend. He'd be lucky to touch his shins, he was pretty sure.

In another smooth motion, she fluidly shifted one leg out to the side and continued a slow series of graceful moves that the three men arrayed in front of her tried to emulate. One was Kyle, a tire carrier, a huge, muscle-bound man Ryder would never in a million years have expected to see trying this. Donnie, a mechanic—lean and a runner, Ryder happened to know—was having more success than his colleague. The third guy, Curtis, was barely trying, too caught up in admiring the view.

But with each one, Hailey demonstrated enormous patience and not one trace of derision that they lagged so far behind her skill.

"I bet she could help even me limber up," Sue Ellen said, craning around him. "Wonder if she'd let me join?"

Ryder did a double take. Sue Ellen practically made a religion out of not exercising.

As if reading his mind, she sniffed. "What, you think I can't do it?"

He held up his hands. "Just don't know why you'd want to."

"If I thought I'd wind up looking like her, I might do a lot of things."

Ryder turned back and observed Hailey awhile longer. Her body was taut, her muscles toned, her lines sleek and elegant. When he saw her move effortlessly into a headstand and hold it, he knew that her grace was deceptive. The woman had to be strong to pull off something like that. She was a contradiction in other ways, he was discovering. He'd never have dreamed that Granola Girl could get so excited at a race, but her eyes had shone, and he'd almost swear she'd been fiercely rooting for Jeb on Sunday.

But then he'd seen her with Brandon when the sponsor came down to congratulate him, and she'd giggled—*giggled*—at something the man had said.

There was no figuring this woman out. Not that he wanted to. "I'll be out for a little bit," he told Sue Ellen.

Sue Ellen only nodded and kept watching.

"DO YOU KNOW WHAT that blasted woman has done?" Greg Schiffer stormed into Ryder's office two days later. "I specifically told her yoga was not part of my training regimen, but she's got my whole crew working out with her in the evenings."

Marcus Conroy smirked from behind him. "She's feeding them lunch, too. She has the guys actually trying tofu."

"If the crew loses one ounce of strength…" Greg's face turned an alarming shade of red. "You have to put a stop to this. She's disrupting everything."

"Yeah, Ryder, what are you gonna do about her?" Marcus chimed in.

"She's not my problem. Talk to Dixon." Ryder turned back to his spreadsheet.

"Oh, yeah?" challenged Marcus. "Did you hear she's teaching Jeb meditation?"

Ryder closed his eyes. Everywhere he turned, it seemed that Hailey was meddling in something, but Dixon was wreathed in smiles every day because she was involved and interested in his people. "I'll talk to her," he muttered.

"When?" Greg demanded. "It's her or it's me, Ryder. You hired me to make your pit crew hum, and I'm doing that."

"She's trouble, yet you haven't lifted a finger to stop her so far," Marcus said, his eyes glinting. "Gone soft, McGraw? Or maybe that's not your problem in regard to her."

Ryder decided then that Marcus was definitely history. He would call Bodie Martin as soon as he returned from checking on Hailey. "I said I'd deal with her." He stalked past both of them. He could be aggravated at Hailey and had plenty of reason to be—the blasted woman had this habit of getting under his skin—but he would not stand for Marcus's oily insinuations about her. He simply had to walk a fine line, that's all, because her presence meant so much to Dixon, as did her happiness. Other people didn't know what he did about the reasons why their normally steely and impassive boss was vulnerable when it came to his daughter.

He headed for the conference room, only to find it empty. The faint notes of some weird music drifted in through the double doors leading to the shop area. He followed them until he reached the break room, only to stop stock-still at the sight before him.

All the tables had been shoved to the side and chairs neatly stacked on top of them. The overhead fluorescents were out, and Hailey had candles—*candles,* for Pete's sake—lit and sitting on the countertops. Some kind of unearthly woo-woo music, all flutes and crap, was playing.

And though his pit crew had had the sense not to be participating when Greg was around, he spotted four mechanics, two fabricators, three engineers and Sue Ellen all lying on mats on their backs like nap time in kindergarten. Every single one of them wore an expression of pure relaxation and peace.

Hailey's head rose, her face serene as she spoke softly in a tone so calming it made Ryder want to sit down and just... breathe.

Oh, man. He tensed to say something, do something—

Hailey only smiled so sweetly at him that his heart gave a little flip.

No. No way. She was not dragging him into her wackiness. He closed his ears to the music and steeled himself against the calming atmosphere, backing out the door quietly while assuring himself that he did not want to give in, not for one second, to the pull of the palpable soothing that swirled in the air.

If his team lost its edge because of Hailey Rogers...

Grimly, Ryder strode back to his office as though the hounds of hell were after him. Once inside, he closed the door, grabbed the phone and punched in the number for Bodie Martin.

Maybe he couldn't easily dismiss one pain in his behind,

but Dixon Rogers didn't love Marcus Conroy. Ryder would wrest back control of at least one part of his life.

And, he reminded himself, Hailey would be gone in less than three weeks.

"YOU'VE CHANGED MY LIFE," Sue Ellen said, hugging her. "I'm sleeping better, after only a few days, and I don't feel so tired after work. Plus when things start getting the better of me, I just do some of that breathing you showed us. My husband Les says he hopes you never leave, and my daughter Tina wants me to bring her to class. My mama looks at me funny, but I can tell she's interested."

Hailey smiled. "They'd be welcome, all of them. Yoga is a lifetime activity. My oldest student was eighty-six."

"I can't get over that I wasn't even that sore after the first day."

"It can be very strenuous, but proper breathing and warm-up help and you—" Hailey glanced over Sue Ellen's shoulder to see Ryder just outside the break room door, his face thunderous. "Uh-oh."

Sue Ellen glanced in that direction, then placed a hand on her arm. "He's under a lot of pressure, honey. But he's a good man. Don't you worry. He won't actually bite your head off." Her gaze shifted. "I don't think." Then she grinned. "I'll talk to him."

"No," Hailey responded more serenely than she felt. "You go on. I'll be fine." She hoped.

Sue Ellen departed with a glare for Ryder as she left. Hailey remained where she was, closing her eyes for a second and inhaling one cleansing breath.

Ryder approached, his gaze locked on hers. He was larger than life, his presence as commanding as his frame. She waited for him to speak, but to her surprise, when he reached her, he only stood silently.

Hailey kept her own eyes on his, seeking to understand the man inside.

He looked tired. Powerful and elementally male as he was, his gaze spoke of a bone-deep exhaustion, a gnawing worry.

Impulsively she reached for his hands. He started in surprise and pulled against her. Though his hands were big enough to swallow hers, she held on, willing some of her own serenity into him.

To her surprise, he hesitated. Let out a deep breath. Deep mossy-green eyes went nearly black as his pupils dilated. Hailey couldn't have looked away if she'd wanted to.

Which she didn't. "Close your eyes," she murmured. "Take a deep breath through your nose. Let your chest expand…feel the breath fill you…let your body relax.…"

For a second, his lids began to drift, his shoulders to lower—

His eyes snapped wide open. He yanked his hands from hers and stepped away. "Don't pull your woo-woo crap on me," he growled.

"You're tired," she said, mustering reason and calm. "I can help you, Ryder. You can't go on at this pace."

"I don't need your help." His brows snapped together.

"I've watched you. You're carrying a killing workload."

"I'm fine." His tone brooked no argument.

He was wrong. She could see it in every line of his frame. She made one more attempt. "If you're too stubborn to let me teach you some coping mechanisms, at least let me give you a massage and work some of the tension from your muscles."

Under other circumstances, she would have laughed at the medley of expressions chasing over his features—shock, insult…and a little bit of intrigue. For an instant, his eyes smoldered.

A lesser man would have stooped to the prurient and focused on the idea of her hands on him, but Ryder McGraw was always rigidly in control. If anything, he stiffened more. "I'm not tense. But you are a problem. Leave my people alone."

A problem. She'd only been trying to help, to find some way to contribute. "No one's forcing them to take a class with me."

"Greg told you no yoga."

"Greg may be the only person around here more rigid than you."

He did a double take. "I'm not rigid."

She rolled her eyes. "If you say so."

He frowned. "I'm not. Running an operation this size, with so much at stake, requires discipline and focus. You're a distraction. We can't afford that."

Maybe she shouldn't feel so hurt, but she did. "I'm trying to help. I—I'm used to working. My father wants me to stay here for a whole month—" she was horrified to hear her voice crack "—and I can't simply sit around and file my nails." Even if she had long nails. Which she didn't. "I'm not doing anything wrong, Ryder. This will help the pit crew, it will help everyone. Not only for flexibility but in dealing with pressure and—"

"We deal with pressure," he interrupted. "We were doing fine before you showed up." He leaned closer, his gaze intent. "Do not mess with my driver. Stay out of his head. You have no idea what you're toying with. If this is some kind of revenge on your father, don't do it. You're hurting more than just him. Not that he deserves it, either."

She was appalled that he would think that of her. "I don't— I wouldn't—"

Ryder shook his head impatiently. He closed his eyes and exhaled. "I believe you mean well," he said with exaggerated patience. "But team chemistry is fragile, and it's everything when you're trying to get to the top of a very competitive field." His gaze actually softened a little. "Look, maybe I can find you someplace off-site to hold your little classes, and you can give them for some of the ladies in town."

Your little classes. Hailey ground her teeth and forgot everything she knew about serenity. "You pompous ass. You're so sure you have all the answers, don't you? Well, there's a big world out there, Ryder McGraw, and for thousands of years before NASCAR or Fulcrum Racing or even the mighty Ryder McGraw existed, people were respecting the body-mind connection and the discipline involved in yoga. They were using it to gain control over their lives and improve the quality of their existence. The world doesn't begin and end in North Carolina or inside this building, much as you seem to think so. But if you want to slap away the hand of someone who's only trying to help, well you just go right ahead, Mr. Know-It-All Crew Chief. As for me, I'll just make myself scarce, never mind that my father wants me involved in his life." She yanked up her yoga mat and her bag and stalked through the door.

Once outside, she looked around her and wondered why she'd ever thought contacting her father was a good idea. She didn't fit here—Mr. Insufferable had made that perfectly obvious. She shouldn't be surprised. Hadn't her mother always said racing was a world unto itself?

It didn't matter, none of this. She wouldn't let it.

So why did she want to sit down right here in the parking lot and cry?

She wouldn't give Ryder the satisfaction. She hadn't fought so hard to achieve serenity, only to let a man who didn't have a clue about her life wreck it. Hailey got in her rental car and pulled out of the parking lot, wondering if this was the last time she'd enter the sacred environs of Fulcrum Racing.

She couldn't think about it right now. *Let go. Breathe. Detach.*

Good advice, she knew.

But at the moment, detachment seemed the most impossible thing she'd ever tried to accomplish.

OH, HELL. RYDER MENTALLY groaned. He'd gone and done it. He was supposed to sell her on racing, not run her off.

Sure, she drove him crazy. And she was disrupting everything.

Especially yourself? an inner voice asked. No. He was fine, just like he'd told her.

Coping mechanisms. He snorted aloud. He coped just fine.

At least let me give you a massage and work some of the tension from your muscles.

Oh, yeah. Like one thing about him would be relaxed with her hands on him. The very thought of those slim fingers on his body…

Do. Not. Think. About. That.

But he couldn't leave matters like this. He had to talk to her, to reason with her, to make her see, as she obviously didn't, how crucial the team's performance was. How many jobs were on the line, if he didn't succeed.

It was what kept him waking up in a cold sweat some nights. Yes, he was competitive. What was wrong with that? Everyone in racing was. They had to be. But now it was all up to him, and the responsibility did weigh heavily on him at times.

Not that he'd ever admit it.

He exhaled in relief that her car was still in the parking lot, though the engine was running. He quickened to a lope.

But when he neared her car, her head was bowed and her shoulders were shaking.

Oh, God. Was she crying? Ryder was renowned for his cool head under intense pressure, but tears…oh, man. Drivers didn't do tears. A little panic skittered through him.

Her head rose, and she wiped her eyes, then reached for the steering wheel.

"No!" He grabbed the door handle and wrenched it open. "You can't drive when you're upset. You're crying. It's not safe."

Her head whipped toward him, then away. "I'm not crying," she said, in a clearly tearful voice. "Go away."

"Look—" He crouched on his heels, so that their heads were nearly the same height. "Hailey, I—" How on earth did he fix this?

"Please get up. Let me be." She reached for the inside door handle.

He didn't budge. "I'm sorry I made you cry."

She stared straight ahead. "I told you I wasn't crying." Then she sniffed.

"Here." He pulled his lucky grease rag from his back pocket, a leftover from his days as a mechanic, and handed it to her. He never felt really complete without a grease rag, though the days when he had an occasion to use one were mostly gone. There was nothing he liked better, though, than tinkering with an engine.

She took it from him, then did a double take. "What is this?"

"A grease rag. But clean, I promise. Blow your nose. Your 'not crying' has your head all stuffed up."

She stared at the rag dubiously, then finally shook her head and used it as daintily as though it was fine linen. She started to hand it back, then held on. "I'll wash it."

"Give it here. That's not the worst thing it's ever had on it."

"I don't mind."

"It's my lucky rag. Please." He held out a hand.

Her lips curved slightly. "Lucky grease rag? Why, Mr. Crew Chief, are you superstitious?"

He flushed and snatched it from her hand, then stuffed it into his back pocket. "Forget I said that," he mumbled.

Her smile widened, and he realized that though she dispensed smiles freely all over the shop, it was the first time since the day they met that she'd smiled at him.

And he was pretty sure he knew whose fault that was. "Have you eaten?" Then he groaned. Like she would want to go anywhere he would eat.

She studied him for a few seconds that seemed much longer. "No. Why?"

He shook his head. "Never mind. It's a stupid idea. You'd hate the places I like."

"I'm not a snob, Ryder. I simply try to take care of my body, and I find that what I eat makes a big difference. It's much like your engines. You wouldn't put substandard fuel in them, would you?"

He sighed. "Here we go again. Never mind." He started to rise.

"Where were you thinking about going?" she asked.

He shrugged. "I have no idea if there's tofu served anywhere in the whole state of North Carolina. I was thinking Maudie's."

"I hear everyone talking about Maudie's. I can find something to eat there, I'm sure."

"I seriously doubt it. The food's great, don't get me wrong. But Sheila runs more to chicken-fried steak than organic fruit."

Her expression seemed wistful, though, so he abandoned thoughts of arguing further. "Your funeral. Come on." He held out a hand to help her alight, then found himself not so eager to let go of it.

He did so anyway. He was only here to extend an olive branch, not do something completely stupid. Even if those words *give you a massage* and the image of her hands on his flesh wouldn't stop dancing around in his head. "My truck's over there."

Her eyes widened as they approached. "All this huge truck for just—" She clapped one hand over her mouth. "I didn't say a word," came from behind muffled lips.

But her expression said volumes.

It means a lot to me for her to like this place and what I do.

Blast you, Dixon. Ryder saw her into the passenger seat, admiring her finely shaped rear as she climbed.

I want you to help me make her feel comfortable.
Fine and dandy. But what about me, boss?
Ryder sighed and rounded the hood of his truck.

CHAPTER FIVE

So this was Maudie's Down Home Diner. Hailey looked around eagerly. Black-and-white tiled floors, red vinyl booths, solid American diner. Maudie's was the real deal, not the glitzy look of the ones she'd seen re-created in California.

She spotted a few familiar faces and was delighted when the guys from the shop waved at her. One of them, Curtis, the parts guy who attended her noon class, rose and threaded his way through the tables. "Hailey! I'm surprised to see you here. Wanna come sit with us?" His grin was wide until he spotted Ryder behind her. "Oh—hey, boss."

"Curtis." Ryder nodded gravely.

"Um, well, uh, you want to join us, Ryder?"

Ryder spared the occupants of the table a nod, then turned back to Curtis. "Thanks, but Ms. Rogers and I have some things to discuss."

Curtis's shoulders slumped. "Okay, sure. But why don't you come over and let me introduce you, Hailey? Just take a second. I've been telling the guys about your class. Would you let folks from other shops join?"

"Of course—" she began.

"No." Ryder's refusal was immediate. "What the hell are you thinking, Curtis? What else are they going to be looking at while they're inside our shop?"

"Oh." Curtis glanced at her apologetically. "Sorry, boss. Wasn't thinking. I, uh, guess I'd better get back to the, uh—" He darted nervous glances between her and Ryder.

"You do that." Ryder's expression was thunderous.

"Thank you, Curtis. It was kind of you to think of me," she said.

"Sure thing." But Curtis's eager smile had completely vanished, and he quickly put distance between them.

"Do you have to do that?" she muttered furiously to Ryder.

"What? Tell the kid to get his head out of his behind and not destroy all our livelihoods? Do you have any idea how slim the margins are between the best teams? Our setups are all unique, and we guard them with our lives. The tiniest advantage can make the difference between success and failure, and those differences are crucial when you're talking hundreds of jobs and millions of dollars."

"But—"

"Hey, Ryder," said the waitress who'd come up to them. She was small with very short dark hair, and above her smile, her eyes held shadows. "Your usual booth?"

"Hi, Mellie. This is Dixon's daughter, Hailey. She's a vegetarian." He said the word like it was a synonym for *plague carrier* or *hardened criminal* or something.

"Oh." Mellie was momentarily nonplussed. "Um, well, we have baked potatoes and salad and, uh, fried okra." There was a nervousness to her that drew Hailey's sympathy.

"Don't worry one bit," Hailey said, touching the waitress's forearm gently. "I hear wonderful things about the food. I'm sure I'll be just fine." Fried...*okra?* She resisted a shudder. She hadn't eaten anything fried in years, and okra...had she ever had that? But she smiled brightly, and Mellie smiled back with relief.

"Right this way."

Many people greeted Ryder, and the respect for him was obvious. As was the curiosity. Something told her he didn't bring women in here often. She settled into the booth and accepted a menu. Immediately she understood that she really wasn't in California anymore.

But she was here to fit in, as best she could, so after

ordering water with a twist of lime, she quickly made selections and told herself that one meal wouldn't kill her. She wasn't rigid.

Unlike someone else she knew. Someone sitting across the booth, still smoldering over Curtis's mistake.

"Ryder, he didn't mean anything, I'm sure."

Ryder shot her a sharp look, but just as he opened his mouth, a couple approached the booth.

"Sorry you missed the auction, Ryder," said Andrew Clark, a friend of her father's she'd met earlier. The older man motioned to the curvy blonde at his side. "Thanks to this woman who refuses to take no for an answer, the Tuesday Tarts made a spectacle of me."

"It was for a good cause." The blonde held out a hand to Hailey. "I'm Grace Clark."

"Hailey Rogers."

"You're Dixon's daughter?"

"I am."

"Well, welcome to the world of NASCAR."

"Thank you," Hailey replied. "What good cause?"

"Children. NASCAR is big on charitable giving of all sorts, but kids are special to all of us. We held a bachelor auction recently and Andrew was a real hit." Then Grace eyed Ryder. "You got away from us this year, Ryder, but we're thinking this will become an annual event, so don't get too comfortable."

Hailey was amused to see Ryder's cheeks color. "Not my thing, Grace."

"Not mine, either," Andrew grumbled. "Coward."

"But you raked in the money." Grace smiled serenely at Andrew, then winked at Hailey.

"I'm not surprised, Mr. Clark," Hailey responded.

"Andrew is fine. And tell your dad he's a chicken, too."

"I will," she promised solemnly, then exchanged grins with Ryder at the very idea. "Maybe."

Andrew Clark laughed and clapped Ryder's shoulder.

"She's a pip. I see why Dixon's so excited she's here. Have a good visit, Hailey." With a grimace, he departed, still arguing with Grace.

"Is that Grace Winters, the celebrity chef?" Hailey leaned across the table.

"It is. Don't get between Grace and anything she's decided she wants." Ryder seemed more relaxed, his expression amused.

Hailey decided to seize the moment. "Ryder, I'd like to learn," she said. "About racing, I mean. I truly didn't come here to cause problems. I want to see the sport through my father's eyes. My mother…" She shrugged.

"Your dad told me she's not a fan of racing."

"My mother is a bitter woman who keeps searching for happiness in places it can't possibly exist. She's never had anything nice to say about racing and blamed Dad's love of it for the divorce, but once I grew up, I realized no divorce is that simple. And now that I'm around my father, I know I'm right. I imagine the traveling can take a toll on a relationship if not handled right, but I have to wonder why she chose not to try. Maybe it was my fault."

He frowned. "You were a child. Lots of families in the sport manage. Some of them home-school and others travel part-time. The season is long and hard, but the guys whose families are involved with the sport have an easier time of it. Whatever happens, though, it's not the kids' fault."

"I wish I understood what happened between them, but my mother won't talk about it, and my father, well…I don't feel comfortable asking him."

"He's real worried that you won't like it here."

"He shouldn't be. Everyone's been very nice."

He tilted his head, skepticism evident. But his lips were curved.

"Okay, some more than others." She smiled right back, and the exchange warmed her.

Ryder raked long, strong fingers through his hair. "It's not you…" he began.

It was her turn to cock one eyebrow. "It is. But I promise I'm not trying to distract anyone, Ryder. It's only…" She lifted her shoulders. "I don't know how to help, and I'm not used to being idle." She leaned forward. "And if you'd be just a little open-minded, there is all kinds of evidence to support my views. Yoga as a discipline is thousands of years old. All sorts of athletes have learned to use it. Why can't it work in NASCAR? If you'd give it a try yourself, you'd see."

He snorted. "Not hardly."

Her ire rose. "You are so—"

Just then Mellie reappeared, and they placed their orders. The break was just long enough to let off some of the steam that had been building inside her.

"It's been years since I got upset like this," she said.

"You don't have to hang around and get upset," he pointed out.

"But I'm trying to learn my father's business."

"No, you're not. You're trying to impose your own views on it. You haven't listened to a word I've said—or anyone else. You just barged in and took over, hijacking a system that's not perfect, no, but we're a new team and we're killing ourselves trying to get better. We were making progress—not steady, not perfectly even, no—but progress. And then you come upset the apple cart."

Hot words sprang to her lips, but Hailey stifled them. Was it true? Such behavior wasn't like her, but if she were honest, she'd felt a need to defend her own lifestyle from the first moment.

Which was the refuge of someone very insecure, as she hadn't been in years—or so she'd thought. "You're right. I'm sorry. I truly didn't realize that's what I was doing."

He seemed stunned. "For real?"

She sighed. "Yes."

They were silent for a moment. Then she leaned forward. "Teach me."

He frowned. "What?"

"I want to learn. Make me, I don't know, an intern or something. Let me be a gofer or whatever. I need to be useful, Ryder. I hate to shop, and I'm not into manicures or highlights. I'm a simple woman who doesn't know her father, and my father's nervous around me. Maybe if I understood better, he'd quit walking on eggshells and we could have some honest discussions, at least about this, which is important to him."

He stared at her. "Then ask him your questions. Let him show you around."

"Ryder, please. Not yet, okay? I'm...well, this is one of the craziest things I've ever found myself saying, but I'm more comfortable asking you. For the next week, at least, would you teach me? Give me things to read or whatever kind of homework I should have. I swear I won't get in the way or be any trouble."

"Oh, and I believe that. Not." He shook his head. "I must be certifiable, but...okay. One week only, though. And if you get in my way, I'm sending you to assist Greg."

"Oooh. Threats. That's mean." But she found herself smiling at him, ridiculously grateful. "I know you're busy. I promise I won't distract you. And I'll wait until you say okay to ask my questions."

Ryder only rolled his eyes and started putting way too much sugar in his iced tea while muttering under his breath.

But his green eyes had the tiniest hint of a grin in them.

So Hailey said not one word about the sugar, as a gesture of good faith. "And in return, I'll give you the massage of your life."

His eyes snapped to hers, but there was no grin in them now. Only a flash of pure heat.

Hailey thought she'd meant it only as a gesture of goodwill, but when she looked at that tough, muscled body and imagined her hands on his skin...

She shivered. And took a big sip of her water.

THE NEXT MORNING, Ryder was still thinking about her. He'd been impressed that she'd actually finished her food and done so without grimacing. Maudie's owner, Sheila Trueblood, had dropped by the table to be introduced, and she'd winked at him while listening to Hailey try to describe her first taste of fried okra, which, apparently, Hailey honestly liked, much to her own amazement.

There'd been a dab of cornmeal on Hailey's full lower lip that had driven him clear out of his mind. And that was without *the massage of your life* ringing in his memory.

"No!" He shook his head and sat up straight.

"Are you okay?" asked the man in the doorway.

"Bodie." Ryder scrubbed his face and rose to shake the man's hand. "Just thinking about setups for this week."

"What's your main worry?" Bodie Martin was a grizzled veteran who could do car setups in his sleep, Ryder was sure. Better than that, Bodie wasn't a prima donna like Marcus, who hadn't dealt well at all with being let go, even though Ryder had done his best to keep things calm.

"The camber of the right front is off for Watkins Glen, but nothing my last guy did can be trusted." Ryder grimaced. "Jeb isn't a big fan of the road courses, anyway, and we need to get this right. I'm glad you're here."

"I'm glad you called me. Shall we go take a look?"

"Man after my own heart." Ryder led him out of the office, wondering where his new intern was on this first morning of her "job." Probably changed her mind—that's what he got for buying in to a sob story.

He heard a trill of laughter as they rounded the corner, and he got his answer.

Brandon Granger was leaning against the wall, intent upon Hailey's every word.

"She's a looker," observed Bodie.

Ryder narrowed his eyes. "Boss's daughter. With our main sponsor."

Bodie's only response was a lift of the eyebrows.

"Ryder," greeted Brandon.

Ryder nodded. "Brandon Granger, this is our new car chief, Bodie Martin. Bodie, this is Hailey Rogers, Dixon's daughter."

The two men shook hands. "You're a legend," responded Brandon. "Pleased to meet you." He stepped back solidly next to Hailey as if staking claim.

Hailey's expression was as much worry as pleasure. "Ryder, shall I follow you?"

"No need to interrupt. You just go right ahead with…whatever you're doing," he responded through gritted teeth.

She was obviously torn, and if he weren't seeing them through the red haze of jealousy, Ryder would admit that she was doing exactly what she should—keeping the sponsor happy.

But why did the sponsor have to be rich, in good shape and obviously taken with her?

"See you," he said as he stalked toward the shop floor.

"That ought to keep the sponsor smiling. Fine little filly Dixon has there. I didn't know he had a daughter."

Ryder ground his teeth. "She's only here for two more weeks." *Which can't pass soon enough.*

"Boss?" Curtis trotted up to Ryder. "Is it true you're making Hailey stop teaching the noon class? 'Cause the guys are pretty worked up over it."

Very aware of Bodie's presence next to him, Ryder bristled. "We need to win, Curtis. Period. Hailey understands."

"She does? Because I don't want to see her hurt." The younger man got those moon eyes he'd had last night.

"Don't you have work to do?" *Don't you remember your screwup last night?* Ryder communicated with a look.

"Um, sure. I'll, uh, get right on it."

Ryder shook his head and moved forward toward the primary car for this week's race.

"What class?" Bodie asked.

"Yoga." Ryder bit off the word.

Bodie's eyes widened. "Yoga? These guys, in this shop?" His grin stretched, too. "There's gotta be a story behind that."

Ryder rolled his eyes. "Needs to be told over a beer."

Bodie chuckled and slapped his back. "Well, for this one, I'm buying." Then he stopped in front of the laptop set up beside the car, and his grin faded in concentration.

After a few minutes of discussion, Ryder called a meeting of the engine builder, mechanic, fabricator and engineer for two hours from now. He set Bodie up with his own laptop at the desk vacated angrily by Marcus first thing this morning, so Bodie could get current.

"I'll be right back," he said. "There's someone I have to talk to." He strode down the hall in the direction he'd last seen Hailey.

HAILEY PRACTICALLY RAN toward Ryder's office once Brandon left, though not before he'd managed to get her to agree to have dinner with him in Watkins Glen. Her father had beamed when he'd heard, so she knew she had no choice. Not that Brandon wasn't a really nice man—he was.

But she'd promised Ryder she'd be at his beck and call, and it was now after 10:00 a.m. and she had yet to report for duty, though she'd been at the shop even earlier than he'd arrived. The look on his face when they'd crossed paths earlier hadn't been promising.

Well, what was she supposed to do? Brandon was the main sponsor, and Ryder had said sponsor money was critical, so—

"Oof!" She smacked right into a very broad chest. Strong hands steadied her. "Ryder. I'm sorry. I was here early, and I didn't expect Brandon—"

"Take a breath," he said. "Isn't that what you teach in your classes?" He was studying her oddly.

She did as he suggested, closing her eyes for a second and wiping her mind clean.

Then she opened them. "What?"

"I didn't cancel your class."

"Oh. I know. I did."

"Why?"

She shrugged. "Because I promised you I wouldn't be a distraction." She forged ahead with the truth. "But actually, I'm hoping to shift the noon class to nighttime, right after…"
Shut your mouth, Hailey.

One dark eyebrow lifted. "After you work with my pit crew, despite Greg forbidding it?"

Don't get upset. Serenity…peace…well-being—

Her eyes snapped to his. "I didn't invite them, they heard about it from somewhere else—and it's only a few. Does Greg control every single thing they do? Do they have to call him before they go out on a date or phone their mothers or—" She clapped her hand over her mouth. She was this close to shrieking like a fishwife. "I've worked very hard to eliminate the sources of anger in my life, and I was doing just fine until—ooh!" She threw up her hands and turned on her heel, ready to leave.

"Hailey." He gripped her shoulder gently. "Cool down. No one's attacking you."

One…two…three… Oh, forget it. She whirled back. "You are. All the time, you are. You glared at me this morning when I was with Brandon, but I was only trying to be polite because you said the sponsor's goodwill is important. You despise everything I value. You dismiss me as though being from California is a crime, even when I humor you and eat fried okra. Fried! Do you know how long it's been since one bit of grease passed my lips?"

"You liked the fried okra," he pointed out.

"You might like tofu, but are you man enough to try it?"

He reared back. "Man enough? Babe, that's not all I'm man

enough to do." Before she could react, he'd pulled her to him, one strong arm around her waist.

And laid a kiss on her that...that...

Oh, my. Hailey's every last thought melted away as Ryder McGraw proved that he was indeed man enough to kiss the socks off her. She didn't want to respond because he was the most annoying, irritating...

Ryder tilted his head and slicked his tongue over the seam of her lips, seeking entrance.

And she couldn't seem to stop her hands from sliding up those muscled shoulders, her fingers from tunneling into his thick black hair. A thrill ran through her, one of pure appreciation for a man who kissed like a dream. He felt good—more than good—against her, and she nearly purred like a cat as she wriggled closer, seeking...

Ryder tore himself away. "Damn."

Damn? She gasped for breath, and noticed that his very broad chest was heaving, too.

"I..." He stared at her, as shocked as she was, apparently, by the impact. His jaw clenched, and he backed away. "I have work to do."

Is that all you can say? But she gathered her dignity and backed up a step, as well. "Of course. So what's my first task, boss?" She would stand her ground and not run, even if he was going to. She could, however, have done just fine without discovering that Ryder McGraw was even sexier than he looked.

"I...I..." For the only time since she'd met him, Ryder seemed at a total loss. He raked one hand through his hair. "Uh, go—hell, I don't know. Go ask Sue Ellen if she needs help with something."

"I'm supposed to be helping you." A little of the devil seemed to have gotten into her. Beneath her shock, she found herself enjoying his discombobulation. She doubted she'd ever see it again.

Unless I can make him kiss me again, came the thought unbidden.

Stop that.

"Stop what?" he asked.

Oops. She hadn't meant to say it aloud. "Nothing. So...I'll see what Sue Ellen needs—*coward*—and then I'll report back to you."

He looked incensed. "I'm not a coward."

"And how do you plan to prove that?" she asked with teasing sweetness, unable to believe this vixen was her. "Want to try that kiss again?" Though the mere thought caused a tremor.

His eyes widened in alarm. "No. Never."

Never? We'll just see about that. But aloud she said, "Then you have one other choice, Mr. Crew Chief."

"What's that?" he asked warily.

"I'll be making tofu for lunch tomorrow. And you'll be eating some."

It was all she could do not to laugh out loud at his expression.

But "Fine" was all he said before he did an about-face and left her.

CHAPTER SIX

HE WAS NOT SIXTEEN. He shouldn't have been reliving one kiss half the night.

Or the feel of that slim, taut body, sleek and yet soft. Those bee-stung lips he craved just one more taste of, to be sure he hadn't overstated their impact.

The team would be leaving for the Glen right after lunch, blast the woman. He didn't usually even eat lunch on travel day, not until he was on the plane, so he didn't waste any time.

But the whole shop was buzzing over Hailey's challenge. Never mind that *he* sure hadn't told anybody.

I swear I won't be a distraction. Uh-huh. Yeah, sure. Thanks, Hailey.

As he walked toward the break room with the dragging stride of a prisoner on a chain gang, Ryder looked around him at the bright eyes and high spirits of everyone in the shop from front office to the loading dock, and realized something startling.

Yes, he was on display, and he hated that.

But even employees who normally had little contact with employees from other parts of the organization were talking to each other, joking around, eager and excited.

Except, of course, Greg, whose face was like a thunder-cloud.

Ryder refused to engage Greg right now, though, and turned away right about the time the room fell quiet and people drifted back from the table where Hailey presided over a buffet.

She had on a little sundress that should have been fairly

modest, except for the fact that it clung to her body in all the right places, leaving no doubt that this was one fine specimen of femininity.

He dragged his gaze from the curves that had cost him more than a few hours of sleep last night and looked at her face.

Her smiling face, alight with challenge.

Beside her stood Dixon, button-busting proud.

Traitor.

Man up, Ryder told himself. *You ate worms when you were a kid. This can't be worse.* But he approached the buffet table as though it was a gallows and Hailey held the noose.

"Hi, Ryder," she said sweetly. Her blue eyes twinkled, and that mouth…

Do *not* look at that mouth. He dropped his gaze to the spread before him.

She gestured to one steaming batch of vegetables and the dish of rice beside it. "Stir-fry with brown rice," she said.

Okay, you eat Chinese. You can do this.

"And this is barbecued tofu." She pointed at a second dish. "Plus coconut and tofu curry. Over here is fruit salad. Organic, of course."

Barbecued tofu? "Of course," was all he said, though.

"And here's your plate. Want me to dish it up?"

"You're enjoying this, aren't you?" he said, pitched so only the two of them could hear.

Her grin was huge. "I am. But you're going to enjoy it, too, I promise."

"You promised you wouldn't be a distraction, either," he said sourly. Then was sorry when her smile vanished.

As an apology, he scooped up a large helping of the stir-fry and rice, then a good-sized one of the fruit. He hesitated over the weird golden-brown cubes purported to be tofu, but then defiantly he slapped a heap of them on his plate, along with the curry, and turned to go.

"You're not going to taste the food here?" she asked.

He glanced back at her, gaze narrowed. "I still have work to do."

Her face fell. Then she recovered. "Well, okay, if you want to be a—"

Coward. She didn't have to say it for both of them to hear it.

He grabbed a fork and plunged it into the curry. "There! Satisfied?" Then he stifled a yelp. "Damn, this is hot!" Tears sprang to his eyes, and he looked around for a glass of water, but his mouth settled as he chewed, and he cocked his head, surprised. "Good that I like things hot," he said, staring straight at her with plenty of meaning behind his gaze.

"So you think it's good?"

The vulnerability he saw made him respond honestly. "The consistency is weird, but…yeah. It's tasty."

Applause broke out, and the rush for the table began. Ryder held Hailey's gaze with his until the crowd swallowed her up. He took a bite of the stir-fry, too, which was, to his great surprise, really good.

Meat would be better, of course, but tofu wasn't the worst thing he'd ever tasted.

Just then a break appeared and he could see her again, so he held up another forkful and showed her that he'd already cleared a third of his plate. He stuck another bite in his mouth, then tapped his forehead in salute.

Hailey smiled, sweet as an angel this time, and something in Ryder's heart twisted a little.

No heart. No distractions. He had a race coming up, and that was all he could afford to focus on now.

He left the room as quickly as possible.

But he did clean the whole plate.

THE TIRE CARRIER, Kyle, gave Hailey a thumbs-up as Ryder called for a pit stop late in the race at Watkins Glen. Hailey bit her lip. So far, the crew had been flawless, and Jeb was third with twenty laps to go. She should have been thrilled that, at a minimum, she hadn't done any damage to the crew's fitness, but instead she twisted her fingers in her lap where she sat in the rear of the pit box, staring at Ryder's broad shoulders.

He sounded the epitome of calm as he gave instructions and chattered with the driver in a cool, measured voice. Everyone looked to him to set the tone for the whole team, to keep them on target and efficiently doing their jobs, meshing the efforts of many people to get what all of them were after: a win.

And now Jeb was close. From what Hailey had learned in the last week, along with noting her father's white knuckles and Ryder's rigid back, Jeb still had time to win this—but only if not one thing went wrong.

Like a pit stop. And she'd been meddling with the crew, the way Greg put it, even though she truly believed in what she was doing.

Jeb's car rolled in and a ballet ensued, a beautifully choreographed dance of strong men with reactions timed down to the millisecond. This would be the last stop, and Jeb's chances hinged on getting out faster than either the first- or second-place cars.

Hailey listened to the count and gnawed on her lower lip.

"Yes!" her father shouted, and even Ryder's tense shoulders eased.

Eleven point eight seconds.

And Jeb crossed the exit line of pit road up one spot.

The guys on the crew who'd been in her class jumped and high-fived each other but settled down quickly at Ryder's command. The race wasn't over yet.

I don't like that I can't see the whole track, Hailey thought. Road courses were different, and right now she was so tense that somehow she thought she'd rest a little easier if she could simply stand and look at the backstretch. She clung to her often-interrupted view of the television coverage while wondering how on earth Ryder withstood the pressure, week in and week out, for months on end—all the time, really, she'd begun to realize. A crew chief's job was never over, even when the season ended.

You just barged in and took over, hijacking a system that's not perfect, no, but we're a new team and we're killing ourselves trying to get better.

She hadn't meant to be a problem, but watching Ryder through a second race helped her see the enormous weight on those very fine shoulders. In that moment, she made a decision that she would cancel all her classes and stay out of his way. She'd come to care for all these people, and though she still believed in the importance of caring for the body and the mind through a discipline that had been her lifesaver, she understood that she was quite likely as rigid as she'd accused Ryder of being.

A collective gasp rose in the crowd, and Hailey focused again on the race, realizing that Jeb was making a bid for the lead, with a hairy curve up ahead. She jumped up and started to reach for Ryder but instead clasped both hands over her chest.

When Jeb made the pass just in time, with half a lap to go, and Bart Branch made a charge to grab first place again, her heart was in her throat. Tension whipped through the pit box like an exposed electrical wire.

But Jeb held the lead, if only by a matter of inches at the checkered line.

"Yes!" Ryder leaped and punched a fist in the air, a very unusual sight from this self-contained man. He turned to her, green eyes alight even as he was talking over the radio, congratulating his driver, and Hailey sighed over his beautiful smile.

Then her father was hugging her, and the pit crew guys swarmed the box and swept her down, cheering.

"Best stops we've ever done!" cheered the catch can man.

"You did it, Hailey! Did we rock or what?" Kyle yelled.

"I didn't do it." But she couldn't stop grinning. "You all did. You were already in superb condition, just a little…tight."

"Well, we're loose now!" Kyle picked her up and twirled her like she weighed nothing.

Hailey was pulled from his arms into those of Brandon Granger, who proceeded to lay a jubilant kiss on her. Hailey reeled in shock, but fortunately she was saved from responding by her father's appearance, back-slapping the sponsor.

Hailey turned away from the melee, only to spot Ryder staring at her oddly. A little shudder went through her at the sudden seriousness, but she pushed it aside and raced toward him. "Congratulations! That was amazing!"

But Ryder pulled back from her. "Thanks." He looked over her head instead. "I have to go to Victory Lane now." He turned on his heel and departed.

Leaving Hailey curiously bereft and hollow.

RYDER CONGRATULATED Jeb, did the hat dance in Victory Lane, granted interviews in the media center. Smiled until he thought his face would break.

But all the while, he was seething inside.

Kiss me, then kiss Brandon Granger, will you? I don't share, Hailey. Do. Not.

He tried to remind himself that she was the boss's flaky daughter, the Granola Girl who would return to California. That they could not be more unlike.

But he kept seeing her eating fried okra and laughing. Taunting him with tofu. And smiling. Moving with a grace that caught his breath.

And clutching his hair in her fingers as she poured herself into a kiss.

It was one stupid kiss, that's all. It should be no big deal. He'd kissed women before. There was no serious woman in his life, but he wasn't a monk.

But, damn it, her kiss was different. At least he'd thought it was. Thought she felt it, too. His cell rang as he stalked back toward the hauler. "McGraw."

"If that fluff brain is giving herself credit for those pit stop times, you and I know better."

Ryder pinched between his eyebrows and sighed. "Hello, Greg."

"I'm not sure I like your tone. You're not buying her garbage, are you?"

"She's not claiming credit—but the guys believe in her. And they were the fastest we've seen all season."

The phone lines went blue from Greg's curses. "She's worked with them for two weeks—against my orders, mind you—and I've been with them since the beginning. My rep is solid, Ryder. Who are you gonna believe?"

"Why are you so threatened by her? She's never done anything to you."

"Never done anything?" Greg practically screeched. "She questions every last thing I do. She's trouble, Ryder, and she doesn't belong here. She'll go on her merry way soon and never give the team another thought—unless she's after Daddy's money, that is. What, she's gotten to you? I mean, she is a pretty piece of—"

"Don't go there, Greg."

As if realizing he'd gone too far, Greg said nothing else.

"I'll see you in the shop next week." Ryder clicked off and continued on his way to the hauler, people giving him wide berth as he walked. He was so lost in thought that he nearly passed it.

"Hey, boss man, gimme five!" The hauler driver was the only person on the team he hadn't seen yet, and Ryder pulled himself out of his funk to smile and comply. "Hell of a race, huh?"

"It was."

"Perfect strategy all the way through."

"Everyone performed at top speed and skill."

"Yeah, but you're the captain, and don't you try to skip out of taking credit." The driver looked past him. "Isn't that right, Ms. Rogers?"

Ryder didn't want to turn around, but he did anyway.

"Call me Hailey, please. I'm sorry to interrupt, but I forgot my tote bag."

"I'll get it for you. They're almost packed up." The driver left them.

Then they were alone, or as alone as they could be at a race track.

"Congratulations, Ryder. He's right. You called a perfect race. Everyone did an amazing job." Her smile was faint, her eyes nervous.

"Especially the pit crew?" he asked.

She drew back as if stung. "I wasn't going to say that. I mean, yes, they were terrific, but everyone was right on the money, best I could tell."

"Greg already called me to be sure you weren't hogging the credit."

She snorted faintly. "Yeah, right." She shook her head. "I don't know why he dislikes me so much."

"He thinks you'll blow us all off the second you leave. Or that you're after Daddy's money."

She took an involuntary step back. "What?" She shook her head. "That's not why—" Her gaze darted to his. "Oh, my goodness, do you think my father believes that?"

She looked so devastated that he couldn't stop himself from reaching for her, Brandon be damned. "I don't believe it, and I'm sure your father doesn't, either. That's just Greg, trying to hurt you."

"But—" The tears swimming in her eyes did him in.

He drew her closer. "You don't deserve that. And no one else will believe it. Forget Greg."

One tear slipped over her lashes, more evidence of the tender heart she didn't even try to protect. She might be headstrong and hold some oddball beliefs, but one thing Ryder was certain of was that there was not a malicious bone in Hailey's body.

"Come on," he urged her, turning her and wrapping one arm around her shoulders. "Let's head for the plane as soon as you get your tote bag. And let me take you to dinner when we get home."

"It'll be late by then, and you've had a long day." She glanced up at him gratefully, then straightened and stepped away. "I'm not weak, Ryder, just because I'm peaceable."

He took her chin and pressed one soft kiss to her lips. "I never said you were." His mouth hovered over hers as he fought the temptation to dive in and take more.

But just then, the driver appeared. "Uh, sorry. Um, here's your bag."

Hailey took it with gracious thanks and scooted off.

Ryder met his driver's eyes with a note of warning to keep what he'd seen private. "Thanks. With our schedules, I won't see you until Michigan. Be safe."

"Will do, boss."

Ryder picked up speed to catch Hailey.

Even if the smartest thing he could do would be to run in the opposite direction.

CHAPTER SEVEN

THE ENTIRE FLIGHT back to Charlotte, Dixon was revved up about the win and kept Ryder engaged in talking over plans for the future beyond this season, something he would normally have enjoyed immensely.

If he hadn't had to watch Brandon Granger sit next to Hailey, monopolizing her every second. The guy didn't even live in Charlotte, he lived in Raleigh. And he had his own damn plane.

By the time they touched down, Ryder couldn't get off the aircraft fast enough. What was up with her? Did she not get how it made him feel?

She might say she was just trying to help out and keep the sponsor happy. He'd buy that if they hadn't been thick as thieves the whole way back.

Or if he hadn't witnessed that kiss at the end of the race.

He didn't need this. He had a job to do. *I need your help,* Dixon had asked.

Looks like she's taken to racing just fine, Dixon. No need for me to spend any more time on a sales job.

All he needed right now was a good night's sleep, but sleep was the last thing on his mind. He glanced at his watch. Maudie's was open for another hour. He was starving, and his refrigerator was empty. He threw his bag into the truck and took off.

Sheila had just placed a glass of iced tea in front of him and was taking his order when her attention shifted. "Hi, there, Hailey."

Ryder didn't swivel to look, but he didn't need to. Hailey

slid into the seat across from him. "May I join you?" Her smile was bright. Too bright.

He shrugged. "Free country."

Hailey ordered a salad—with a side order of fried okra, he noted—then Sheila departed.

He said nothing.

"I really like Sheila, don't you?" When he only grunted, Hailey's fingers twisted on the tabletop. "She's young to have created such an impressive business."

"Why are you here, Hailey?"

"I'm not sure." Her gaze darted over the room and back. "That's not true. Why did you kiss me? Again?" Her tone held a note of…what, aggravation?

"Beats the hell out of me."

Then she looked hurt. "Ryder, don't toy with me."

He goggled at her. "Toy with *you?* Who is it that's playing footsie with Brandon Granger every time I turn my head, then kissing me as though you liked it?"

"I'm not playing anything with Brandon," she huffed. "You said it's important to keep the sponsor happy."

He stared at her. "That means producing as a team, promoting the sponsor's product, conducting ourselves in a responsible manner to not besmirch the sponsor's image." He slapped his palms on the table. "It does not mean acting like a hussy."

Her mouth fell open. "Hussy? You're calling me a…a…" She leaped from the booth. "You are the biggest jerk I've ever met in my entire life."

She threw down her napkin and practically ran from the diner.

"Hailey!" Swearing, he rose and charged after her.

"Wait!" he shouted as she slammed her car door shut and cranked the engine. She began to back out of her parking spot, and he was left with a dilemma—let her go and make Dixon furious that he'd upset her or try to stop her when she wanted nothing to do with him?

The parking lot only had one exit on this side of the diner. Ryder made a split-second decision and loped full-out to beat her to it. For whatever reason, he couldn't kid himself that he was more than intrigued by her. More attracted than was sensible, but he kept discovering new facets to her.

And she sure hadn't deserved that insult. She was no hussy, and she was right—he was a jerk to have unloaded on her. When he planted himself in the middle of her only way out, he wondered if she might not just keep coming.

Not that he might not deserve it. He'd worked hard to always be in control of himself, but when his temper was aroused, he had a tendency to go off half-cocked and say things he regretted later. Ergo why he kept it within his rigid grasp.

If he was honest, Hailey got to him on too many levels. He could tell himself that he was out here to stop her because Dixon would be upset, but Ryder wasn't in the habit of lying to himself. What had really gotten to him was her stricken look when he'd used that stupid word.

Ryder had the sickening feeling that he was beginning to find Hailey Rogers way too compelling. A relationship with someone local, given his hours, would be difficult; to have one with someone three thousand miles away…better nip any foolish thoughts in the bud.

He heard her engine as she rounded the row and headed straight for him. He was almost certain she'd stop—of course Granola Girl would stop.

But she didn't do it quickly. She actually gunned her engine for a few feet.

Damn, every time he thought he had a bead on her, she surprised him.

Well, he was about to surprise her. The second she slammed on the brakes, he was at her door and yanking it open. He leaned in, unbuckled her seat belt and pulled her to her feet.

"I'm sorry, all right?" Her shocked expression made him

smile. "I was…I was just…" He lowered his head to hers, and above her lips, he finished his sentence. "Oh, hell, I was jealous. Feel better?"

Then he proceeded to indulge in a scorching kiss, pressing her body all along the front of his, the way he'd been dying to do for days.

As the kiss ended, Hailey drew back, but he didn't let her go far. "I don't understand you," she said, her pupils huge and dark.

He laughed. "Join the crowd. I don't understand you, either. But man, do I want you." And he dove in for another taste of her.

Hailey rewarded him with a softening of her frame against him, tempting him to make an even bigger spectacle of himself than he already had. He didn't need to see the eyes peering out from Maudie's to know that word would be all over NASCAR before dawn that Ryder McGraw, Mr. Serious, had lost his mind.

"I don't care," he muttered.

"What?" She blinked, her expression dazed.

"Nothing. Just kiss me. Come home with me, Hailey. I'm dying here." He let his hands and his lips demonstrate the depth of his desire for her.

"But—"

"But nothing." Before she could think straight, he had her around the car and buckled into the passenger seat and was headed for the driver's door when he remembered that they'd ordered food that hadn't arrived. "Wait here. Do not move."

Faster than he'd ever crossed a distance before, he made it inside the door of Maudie's and was throwing bills at Sheila. "Keep the change."

"Well, Ryder McGraw, I do declare—"

Ryder didn't wait to hear what she'd say. He'd have days ahead to hear about this.

But he and Hailey had been dancing around each other

since the day she'd set foot inside Fulcrum Racing. This wasn't going to solve anything, taking her home with him.

But if he had anything to say about it, they were both going to feel very good in the morning.

And everyone who knew Ryder McGraw understood that whatever he set his mind to was gonna happen.

WITH EVERY BLOCK, Hailey grew more nervous. Whatever rush to her head his kisses had created, she was stone-cold clear now. "I can't do this."

"What?" His gaze snapped to hers, then back to the traffic.

"Ryder, turn around. You said you believed I'm not a hussy. What does going home with you make me?"

He stopped at a light and studied her. "You're from California."

"So?"

"That's the most old-fashioned thing I think I've ever heard a grown woman say."

"Why? Because it's you we're talking about me going home with?"

He recoiled. "No, of course not. But…Hailey, we're adults. We're single and unattached—at least, I am." He appeared startled by the notion. "Are you involved with someone?"

"Not really."

"Not really? What does that mean? Either you are or you aren't." His jaw flexed. "I don't poach on other men's women."

Hailey had to chuckle at his expression of affront. "Who's old-fashioned now? Other men's women? Women are not possessions, Ryder."

"Don't change the subject. Are you involved with someone?"

She shrugged. "There's a fellow instructor I've gone out with several times, but—"

"But what?"

She hunched her shoulders. "He wants to get serious. I won't do that."

"What do you mean *won't do that?* What do you have against getting serious?"

"The light's changed," she pointed out.

He touched the gas again, but only long enough to round the corner and park the car. "Talk to me, Hailey."

"I'd rather not."

"You don't ever want to get married, is that it? No husband, no kids?"

She pursed her lips. "I want them." Wanted them badly— but not badly enough to risk making her parents' mistake.

"Is it because of your parents' divorce?"

She didn't want to discuss the topic. "Let me drive, Ryder. I'll take you back to your truck. It's been a long day, and I'm sure you're tired."

"Not that tired." He cast her a grin that, in the lights from the dashboard, seemed positively devilish.

Her heart gave a little skip. *Slow down, girl. There's no future with this one.*

Which, now that she considered it, was perfect. She glanced sideways and took inventory. All man, with that rugged jaw, the five o'clock shadow, the firm mouth. Eyelashes so long women would kill for them, slashing dark brows, strong nose...and that was just the face.

Ryder's body...yum. Tall and well-muscled with hands... oh, my...she was a real sucker for a man's hands, and his were just right. Long fingers, wide palms, strong wrists...now it wasn't her heart skipping, but a tug much deeper within her.

Quickly, she faced front again, searching in the headlights for signs of where they might be. They passed a sign for Lake Norman, an area where many drivers and owners had lake-shore properties and huge mansions, but Ryder kept going.

"Where are we?"

"Nearly there. Another ten minutes."

She was surprised. He was such a workaholic that she

would have assumed he'd live near the shop. "A long way," she commented.

A cock of his head. "I know. I spend so much time at the shop, I wonder why I bother, but—" he shrugged "—I like to get away when I can."

Down a solitary road, winding through a virtual forest until Hailey knew she'd never find her way home.

Her father's house, she corrected. She wasn't sure where home was. And she wouldn't be in Charlotte much longer. Nearly halfway done.

How much had she actually achieved in her quest to reconnect with her father? She'd learned that he was a good man and a kind one; she was glad to know that her mother's tales of his faults had been severely overstated. Maybe he had been a workaholic and put racing first as her mother insisted, but even if that were true, he wasn't that man now. He couldn't do enough for her; daily she had to turn down overtures from him for a new car or new clothes or jewelry, all of them attempts, she was sure, to respond to what many women treasured.

But every single one only highlighted that her father didn't really know her, that they hadn't truly connected. Nice as he was being, their constant tiptoeing around each other was tiresome.

Ryder McGraw might disapprove of her, might wish her to vanish—well, maybe not now, but certainly for most of her visit—but she never had to wonder where she stood with him.

"Here it is," he said just then, yanking her from her musings. "Not much to look at."

Hailey's eyes widened. On the contrary, this place was more to her liking than anything she'd seen since her arrival. She didn't say anything at first, only alighted from the car and wished it were daylight so she could see more.

A simple log cabin and a wide porch with two rockers on it. No landscaping to speak of, a crushed stone driveway and front walk. She followed Ryder up to the steps, turning around to see tall trees encircling this clearing, the stars bright as she hadn't seen them since Santa Fe, the moon bathing the entire scene in a soft white glow.

"It's beautiful," she said. And it was, all of it. Oh, she could envision hanging baskets spilling over with blossoms, shrubs and flowers skirting the porch and continuing down the walkway... "It's...Ryder, it's perfect."

She turned back to see him regarding her differently than before. "What?"

He shook his head. "Nothing." He shrugged. "I just—I figured you'd think it was too primitive."

"Well, you'd think wrong." She brushed her fingers over one of the rockers, sturdy and very old, judging by the paint flecks clinging to weathered wood.

"My grandfather made those for my grandmother," he said. "I can still see her sitting in one, shelling black-eyed peas and laughing up at him. I spent a lot of each summer with them up in the mountains of east Tennessee." His usually stern face softened as he gazed into the past.

"You loved them."

He nodded. "They were important to me. These rockers make me feel connected to them still." His hand stroked the top of the same rocker she'd been touching.

"I never had grandparents," Hailey said. "I envy you."

"Never?"

"My mother was estranged from her family, and my dad's folks died before I was born."

"So it was just you and your mom? Where was she from?"

"Iowa. She couldn't wait to get away from the cornfields. California suits her."

"You, too, I guess."

It was Hailey's turn to shrug. "I don't really belong anywhere." He was studying her too closely, and his perusal made her uncomfortable. "May I see inside?"

"Not yet," he said, taking her hand and drawing her nearer.

He slid one arm around her waist and pulled her body against his, then lowered his head to barely brush his lips over the side of her throat.

Hailey shivered. "Ryder…"

"Hmm?" He continued cruising down her neck, pausing at a spot that made her quiver. He halted, his warm breath bathing her skin until she thought she would scream if he didn't hurry up and—

What? Why would she want him to hurry? Except that—

"You're thinking too much," he murmured, his mouth grazing her skin once more, at last, at last, at last…

"I must not be doing this right," he said.

Hailey closed her eyes and dug her fingers into his muscled arms. If he did this any more right, she'd, she'd—

He ranged back across her shoulder to the hollow of her throat where a moan escaped her. She heard him chuckle, felt his mouth curving against her skin, but just as she thought she might have recovered the power of speech, his kisses started up again, this time crossing to the other side with similar results that had her back arching, the center of her body pressing against his very eager one.

Very eager. Very…oh, my…

Hailey's knees gave way.

Ryder swept her up in his arms and locked his mouth on hers in a kiss so blatantly carnal that all she could think was—

More. More, more, more, more…

Vaguely she heard the screen door open, listened to him swear as he fumbled for his keys and unlocked the door. But all she could manage was to sigh and moan and range her hands over that body of his.

He kicked the door shut.

Hailey couldn't touch him enough, couldn't get close enough, then he was kissing her again and every nerve in her body seemed attuned to his slightest touch, breath, taste…

"No thinking," he muttered.

"I can't—"

His mouth closed over hers again.

With a deep, heartfelt sigh of pure pleasure, Hailey complied.

CHAPTER EIGHT

RYDER AWOKE SLOWLY for a change. Never had a night's sleep felt so good. He was tempted to simply lie there and fall back into the last dream where he and Hailey—

Hailey. His head swiveled on the pillow.

There was an indentation in the one next to him.

He sat up. He could smell her scent. He brushed one hand over her pillow in a gesture so foolish he was glad no one had seen it. Memories tumbled in, and he knew they weren't dreams at all, but were instead snapshots of the night just passed.

Sweet mercy. He hadn't had much sleep at all, he realized now. They hadn't been able to keep their hands off each other.

But not one morning of his life had he ever felt better.

He rose and belatedly recalled that he wasn't fully dressed. He smiled.

Quite a night. Quite a woman.

Then he frowned. So where was she?

He started to prowl through the house as he was—he had no neighbors, so it wasn't like he'd scandalize anyone—but then decided that if she were still here, he didn't know her well enough to predict how she'd react.

Though, he thought with another smile, her reactions last night had been perfect.

He frowned again. Perfect wasn't good. He didn't need the Granola Girl being perfect. She wasn't, really. She was stubborn and driven and wanted her own way on everything.

Which, he had to grin as he drew on some basketball shorts, made her remarkably like himself, he supposed.

Except he was sensible and she was anything but.

He stretched and yawned, then struggled his way into the kitchen.

Where a full pot of coffee greeted him. He poured himself a mug. Well, well. She didn't consume, even hated caffeine, so how would she know to make it? But at this point, any caffeine was—

He sipped.

Maybe the best cup of coffee he'd ever tasted.

Ryder frowned again. Not perfect. Not best.

Not Hailey. No, no, no…

Then he spotted her through the window, curled up in his grandmother's rocker, eyes closed, slowly rocking, one long leg and slender foot sticking out from the tail of his shirt, the one he'd been wearing last night.

She looked damn good in it, too. Good enough to start thinking about working her right out of it again.

Down, boy. He couldn't tell what she was thinking, only that she looked at peace, so he settled back against the counter and drank his coffee while he watched her.

And tried not to think about how perfect she looked on his porch. In his rocker. In his shirt.

In his life?

I don't really belong anywhere.

But somehow she seemed to belong right here, in his bed, in his arms…

She's only visiting, Ryder reminded himself. And it was only one night.

Even if it had been the most remarkable night of his life.

Oh, Miss Hailey, you are one very dangerous distraction.

One I absolutely cannot afford.

Ryder glanced at the clock and knew that by now he'd normally have put in two hours at the shop already. He had a lot to do to get ready for Michigan next weekend. There was no time to waste staring at a woman's ankle or her shapely thighs...those lips that had driven him crazy, marking every inch of his body....

A part of him rebelled. What was so wrong with taking a little of this beautiful morning simply to enjoy? To spend a few more moments kissing Hailey?

Because, he reminded that traitorous impulse, *a lot of people are counting on you to build on yesterday's win.*

And Hailey wasn't for him, however much she tempted him.

Visiting. Just visiting. Gone in under two weeks.

For the first time in years, Ryder found himself resenting the demands of his job, and that scared him more than anything else could.

With a sigh, he swallowed the rest of his coffee and went to take a shower.

One very cold shower, coming up.

THE SOUND OF THE SHOWER running broke Hailey's reverie, and she couldn't help tensing, wishing she'd put on her own clothes instead of donning his shirt. But she'd inhaled his scent and yielded to the impulse to be closer to him than she dared be to the sleeping man inside.

Now she wished she could just vanish into thin air. The urge to flee was strong. What had she been thinking, coming home with him last night?

Sex with a gorgeous man—girl, don't kid yourself.

The thought brought a smile. He was gorgeous, that was for sure. Memories rose like champagne bubbles, snippets of pure bliss at the hands of a man who really knew his way around a woman's body.

Who would have guessed that the very driven and serious crew chief would turn out to be such a skilled lover? Though, as she pondered it, the intense focus he brought into everything he tackled should have alerted her. Ryder McGraw believed to his core that anything worth doing must be done with the greatest of effort and concentration.

Her body warmed like honey in the sun as the night replayed on the insides of her eyelids. *Lawsamercy*, as Sue Ellen would say.

"What's so funny?" he asked.

Hailey jolted and leaped from the rocker, staring at him like a deer caught in headlights. She tripped on one board of the porch and grabbed at thin air.

Ryder was there in an instant to steady her, and his touch rippled through her.

She didn't say a word. Couldn't.

Neither did he.

For a few long seconds, their gazes locked and their bodies warmed, instinctively leaning toward the other as plants seek the sunshine.

Until Ryder's cell phone went off.

He backed away as he fumbled in the holster attached to his belt. "McGraw." A pause. "Yes, Dixon. Her phone's turned off. She's with me." His shoulders stiffened. "We'll be there soon."

Hailey closed her eyes. She was a grown woman, but at that moment, she felt like a fifteen-year-old caught late for curfew. She scooted past Ryder's back, scooped up her clothes and headed for the shower.

Regretting the night and her poor judgment.

Every bit as much as she savored every minute of memories.

THE TRIP BACK TO town passed in silence.

Ryder wondered what she was thinking, but the fact that she hadn't spoken one word to him this morning didn't bode well for her reaction to the night that had, for him, been so unforgettable.

And knowing they'd been caught by her father, like two truant teenagers, didn't help his mood, either. He was fairly certain seducing the man's daughter hadn't figured in Dixon's request to make Hailey feel comfortable with the racing scene.

Hell. He hadn't felt this stupid or all thumbs since he *was* a teenager, and he still had to get through reclaiming his truck at Maudie's and encountering everyone at the shop.

He frowned and tapped his thumb on the steering wheel, punching the accelerator, so ready to get this trip over with.

"I'm sorry," Hailey said quietly. "I shouldn't have—it's my fault."

He turned to her. "What's your fault?"

She shrugged. "Everything. It was a big mistake."

Mistake? The word shouldn't hurt. Yes, the whole thing was a mistake on many levels, not one bit wise.

But it had still been one of the best nights of his life. He wasn't going to say that, though. Ryder McGraw didn't do vulnerable. "What's done is done," he said tightly. "I'll take the blame with your dad."

She shot him a quick look he couldn't decipher. "No. You have to work with him, and I won't complicate your life any more than I already have."

"You're his daughter."

It was her turn to shrug. "He'll probably forgive me as long as I promise never to do anything so stupid again. And if not, well, he's lived a long time without me. He'll get over it."

Anything so stupid. Well, that just put him in his place, didn't it? Ryder ground his jaw and focused on his driving. "I don't hide behind a woman's skirts. I'll take my lumps." With relief he saw Maudie's up ahead and pulled into the parking lot. He found a spot near his truck and emerged, then forced himself to do as he'd been raised and go to her door and open it for her.

Her big blue eyes caught him. "Ryder…" She placed one hand on his forearm. "I…"

"Weird to see you here this time of day, McGraw. That win go to your head?" The speaker was none other than his fired car chief, Marcus Conroy, and his gaze shifted back and forth between Ryder and Hailey. "My, my, my...wonder what Daddy will think?"

"Beat it, Marcus," Ryder growled.

"I don't work for you anymore. I don't have to listen to you."

Ryder pointedly ignored the man and turned his attention back to Hailey, but too late.

"I'm sorry," she murmured and slipped past him. The second she was back inside her vehicle, she started the engine and drove off.

"Not such a good night, lover boy?" Marcus taunted.

Not to go for the man's throat required the greatest of effort, but Ryder was late enough getting to work.

But it sure was tempting.

CHAPTER NINE

THE REST OF THE WEEK was pure misery. More than once,
Hailey started to pack her bags. She'd been right; her father
had gone easy on her, but the situation was awkward. Maybe
it was just that Ryder was his employee or maybe any father
had qualms about his daughter having sex. Regardless, she
feared that she'd confused and disappointed him.

What surprised her was how much doing so hurt, though it
was difficult to measure in light of how much worse Ryder's
blatant dismissal of her felt. He acted as though she were invisible, and everyone else at the shop was so uncomfortable that
she'd quit going there altogether. She'd canceled her classes
and had even done little yoga herself, something that would
have been unthinkable B.R.

B.R. Before Ryder. That's how she thought of it. Before
she'd gotten the crazy idea that there was something between
them, when it obviously had only been a simple physical reaction to a virile man.

Every time her mind strayed toward his cabin and that
lovely porch, to say nothing of the incredible lovemaking
they'd shared, she yanked it right back. Sex, that was all it
had been. Scratching an inexplicable and very foolish itch.

She'd clearly lost her mind, or certainly any fragment of
good sense.

"Hailey?"

She looked up from the dinner she'd barely tasted, to see
Brandon's concerned gaze.

Yes, Brandon. He'd stepped right into the breach left by
Ryder's withdrawal. They'd had dinner together three of the

five nights that had elapsed since her disastrous night with Ryder, and he'd offered to fly her on his plane to the race at Michigan. She did want to attend the race for her father's sake, and not having to be anywhere near Ryder would be a relief.

But it also made her feel like a coward.

"Have you decided about the race? We'll be wheels up at 10:00 a.m. tomorrow."

Tomorrow was Saturday. Everyone, including her father, had already left, though he'd done so reluctantly. Hailey passed each hour by thinking wistfully about what the various team members were doing right now. How they were getting along.

Except Ryder, of course. Him, she wouldn't spare a second's thought for.

Sure thing, Hailey. You just keep telling yourself that.

Well, if she didn't have the control she wanted yet, she would keep working on it. The first step might be accepting Brandon's invitation. "I'd love to." She summoned a smile to meet his delighted one.

"We'll have a great time, you'll see. I'll have my pilot fly us into Chicago for dinner at this great little place I know, and I'm having brunch catered in my suite on Sunday before the race. You'll enjoy watching the race from up there."

But I won't see how my guys are doing, she thought. *There will be glass between me and the race and—*

No, not Ryder. She wasn't thinking about him.

Not at all.

"Boy, you have got some kind of bug up your butt," growled Bodie Martin during the final practice session at the track on Saturday. "You going to get your head in the game or not?"

Ryder barely resisted the urge to snap back.

Except he knew he was in the wrong. All week, everyone had been tiptoeing around him like he was a coiled rattlesnake.

Which wasn't too far off from how he felt.

"I'm fine."

"Uh-huh. I've noticed. So has everyone else."

"Bodie…"

"Son, I know you got woman trouble, and there's nothing worse to mess with a man's head, but in case you hadn't noticed, the whole team is tight as a tick, and that's not good for anyone."

"I don't have woman trouble."

"Whatever you say." Bodie returned his attention to the laptop screen.

Ryder exhaled loudly. "All right. I've been a total ass all week. But I haven't neglected my duties."

The older man snorted. "Uh, no. I'd say that's the problem. Have you had four hours' sleep any one night since you got back from the Glen?"

No. Especially not Sunday night, when he'd been too busy making love—having sex, he corrected—with the woman who couldn't get close enough to his sponsor now. And didn't have the guts to face him.

"I said I'm fine," he snapped. "Now read me those lap times again."

Bodie shook his head. Apparently thinking better of commenting again, though, he called off numbers instead.

Ryder dove into the numbers and tried once more to shoehorn himself into a mental place that had once been second nature.

Until he heard the sound of Hailey's laughter. His head jerked up, and his gaze arrowed straight to her. Laughing, yes. And beautiful as ever.

She was also clinging to the arm of the man who could cripple Ryder's team if Ryder mismanaged this by hauling off and planting his fist in the too-pretty mug of the man who shouldn't be touching his woman.

Whoa. Not his woman. Not that he even wanted her to be. Ryder yanked his attention back to the laptop screen that was flooded with gibberish. *Focus, damn it. She's just a woman. The world is filled with them.*

Then, with the snap of a steel trap closing, Ryder McGraw summoned his legendary self-control to banish everything but Jeb's car and the Michigan race from his mind.

AFTER SHE'D BATTLED the covers all night as she recalled Ryder's scowl at seeing her, Hailey finally gave up on sleep at 6:00 a.m. and walked out onto the balcony of her hotel room. The horizon held the faint glow of the rising sun, and Hailey sought refuge in the discipline that had so often brought her peace in the past.

"Greetings, my friend," she murmured to the sun as she slid into the familiar rhythms of the sun salutation. She closed off her mind to any other thought but moving through the paces and relishing the stretch of her muscles as they warmed and once again rewarded her with the sense of well-being she had been missing for days.

She chanted her mantra and let the vibrations of her voice and the healing breaths take her away from anything but how good it felt to inhabit her body, to let her blood flow swiftly and smoothly with her unspoken intentions to be well, to spread her peace to others, to simply let go and…exist. Not think, not worry, not regret, only…be.

With every movement, she found herself unwinding, letting go of the cold, sad knot at her core. When she reached the end of her routine, she settled to the floor and let the sun's warming rays and the rising flood of color suffuse her heart, ease her mind and strengthen her body.

After her meditation ended, Hailey rose and went to shower and dress. She would enjoy this day with her father and Brandon, she would smile at the team and let them know her troubles were past, she would go back to her classes if she could find another place to hold them for the slightly more than a week she had left.

And she would even smile serenely at the man who did not

deserve to unsettle her. She had allowed it to happen, but it would not happen again.

When it was time to depart from North Carolina and her father's life, she would know that she had not allowed a foolish fancy to wreck a serenity that had been years in the making.

LAP 160, AND RYDER knew every person on the team was wondering how this race could get any worse. Two blown pit stops, a brush of the wall and a spin that had nearly sent Jeb into his teammate had all contributed to a very frustrating day for the No. 464 team.

He knew how it could get worse, though. Lousy mental focus could wreck Jeb, and the team was snakebit already. Relentlessly, Ryder kept his voice calm and talked the whole team down from the ledge once again.

"This car is a lost cause," Jeb snapped. "I might as well just drive it into the garage right now."

Ryder didn't react. Yes, his stomach burned like he'd dunked it in an acid bath, but when he spoke, it was with an even tone. "We'll add a round of wedge next time. Three laps until your last stop. You're doing fine, Jeb. Just keep digging."

"What the hell do you think I've been doing all day?" Jeb said tightly. Normally unflappable himself, even Jeb was spooked by how many mistakes they'd made, and being in thirtieth wasn't helping his mood.

"I know you have," Ryder said. "I haven't gotten you the car you need, but nobody's giving up, Jeb. Just hang in there. Anything can happen in the laps that are left."

That much was true, but what was also true was that every bit of the brimming confidence the team had possessed after last week's win had evaporated as if it had never existed.

And Ryder knew who was responsible. The buck stopped with him, even when he wasn't in the wrong—but this time, he was totally at fault. He'd allowed his emotions to get the better of him all week long—and over something as unimportant as a woman, that was the hell of it.

No more. Hailey Rogers would not claim one more second of his time or attention.

He adjusted his headset and hunkered down. "Your lap time was only a tenth of a second behind the leader that go-round, Jeb. I let you down, bud, but I promise you it won't happen again. Listen up, everyone, this race has been a rough one, but it's all on me, and it ends here. Let's finish this one out the very best we can, and know that we've seen the worst for this season or any other one. This will not ever occur again, I promise you."

The silence on the radio was resounding, but Ryder could sense from the easing of postures in the pit box with him and on the ground below that they were listening. That he'd done what he needed to, which was to take any blame off the shoulders of his team and give them a chance to get optimistic again.

He meant it, too. His lapse was unforgivable, and he would never repeat it.

"Let's show the fans thirty-nine laps of top-notch racing, folks."

He saw the nods and heard the murmurs of agreement. He wouldn't forgive himself, but they had.

Now to live up to the confidence they demonstrated in him.

HIS RESOLVE HELD the team together through the race, and Jeb managed to pick up four spots, finishing twenty-sixth. Ryder called the team together at the end and told everyone to go find their favorite way to relax, forget this lousy race and show up on Tuesday ready to kick some serious butt at Bristol.

He even sent away the guys who normally packed up the hauler and asked the hauler driver to come back in thirty minutes. Then, methodically, he did the grunt work, losing himself in shoving heavy toolboxes back up into their slots, letting out his frustrations with himself on mute metal.

He didn't deserve to be a crew chief if he couldn't control himself better than he had this week. Damn it, didn't he know better?

"I want you to help me make her feel comfortable, Ryder," he mocked.

"Talking to yourself?" The insidious tone of Marcus Conroy had him grinding his teeth. "Can't say I blame you. Ready to admit you're not crew chief material? Dixon should have promoted me, and everyone knows that now."

"What are you doing here?" Ryder looked up and saw Marcus's smirk. "How'd you get on the track? Your hard card's been revoked."

"Ah…guess you havn't heard. The No. 593 team just hired me to be the new crew chief." Another smirk. "Though I imagine Dixon's regretting giving in to you now and firing me. I just might wind up with your job after all. You know this disaster is your fault, all because you couldn't keep your hands off of a mere piece of tail."

Ryder wheeled on him. "You don't talk about her like that."

"Ooh, boy's got it bad for the boss's daughter," Marcus taunted. "Not enough to have the top job, now you want Daddy's money, too?"

Ryder took a step toward him, forming a fist.

Marcus backed up and stumbled, then fell.

Ryder yanked him back up by the collar. "Do not ever speak of her again. Now get the hell out." Not hiding his contempt, Ryder released Marcus and began to turn back to his work.

Before he could, Marcus lashed out and nailed Ryder in the side.

Ryder's breath escaped in a gust. He came up swinging and landed a blow squarely on his opponent's nose.

"Stop it!" came Hailey's voice.

"Go away, Hailey." Ryder didn't take his eyes off Marcus,

so he didn't see Hailey move to get between them just as Marcus threw another punch.

It hit Hailey's shoulder instead and knocked her back with a cry.

Ryder grabbed hold and steadied her, then launched himself right at Marcus. "You worthless bastard—"

They both hit the ground hard.

"Ryder!" Hailey cried.

In a haze of fury, Ryder ignored her and reared back to punch the man beneath him. "You will pay for that."

"Ryder, please. I'm okay."

"I'm okay, Ryder," Marcus mocked.

For a solid moment, Ryder locked gazes with him.

Then he shoved to his feet. "You're not worth it." He sought out Hailey, who was watching him with wide, dark, horrified eyes. "Are you hurt?" he asked her.

Before she could answer, Dixon Rogers showed up, with Brandon right behind him. "What's going on here?" He glanced at his daughter. "Hailey? Are you all right?"

Her face was ashen. "I...I think so."

"Sit down, honey." Dixon settled her on the truck's bumper and rounded on Marcus. "I saw you hit her. I can see to it that you never work in racing again."

"It was an accident. And he's the one who lost his cool and blew the race." Marcus turned to Ryder. "I told you she was a distraction that would cost the team. You go falling for her and look what—"

Ryder took another step toward him.

"Perhaps we should call security," interrupted Brandon, who stood at Hailey's side, his arm wrapped around her waist.

Ryder burned to see it, but he kept his distance. None of this was good for his team, however much he wanted to grind Marcus into the asphalt. With extreme effort, he restrained the urge to go after him again. "Leave now and save your new job, Marcus. For a while, at least. You'll screw it up anyhow."

"Why you—" Marcus took a step toward Ryder.

"Conroy!" Dixon barked. "Leave. Now."

Marcus scowled. "You haven't seen the last of me, Ryder McGraw. I'll have your job yet, you just wait." But, like the coward he was, Marcus slunk away, muttering.

Ryder watched him go until he was out of sight.

"We'll talk tomorrow, Ryder," Dixon said ominously. "I want to get her checked out."

Ryder turned around just in time to see Dixon's frown and Brandon's scowl as they led Hailey away.

CHAPTER TEN

"IT'S JUST WRONG," Sue Ellen muttered on Tuesday. "No one caught the fight on camera, no reporters were around, no fans saw a thing."

"What are you talking about?" Hailey asked as she entered the Fulcrum office.

Sue Ellen whirled. "Oh." She shook her head. "Nothing."

"Sue Ellen, did you hear that Ryder got fined—oh." Curtis rounded the doorway and halted at the sight of Hailey.

"Fined? Why?" Then the reason for the uncomfortable looks hit her. "Because of the fight? But he was—" *Defending me.* She'd heard enough as she'd approached on Sunday to know that Marcus had been taunting Ryder over catching the two of them together in Maudie's parking lot after their night together.

"Are you okay, hon?" Sue Ellen asked.

"I'm fine." She pressed her lips together. Did they know? *Of course they did.* Probably most of NASCAR had heard the gossip by now. "Ryder was taking up for me. That's not fair for him to be punished."

"He's not even appealing. He's beating himself up, yes, for yet another distraction for the team," Sue Ellen said. "But he's not blaming anyone but himself."

"When he should be blaming me." Hailey looked away. *Yet another distraction.* Ryder had accused her of being one before. It seemed like she presented nothing else, no matter how hard she tried. "I don't belong here." She started for the door.

"This isn't your fault, Hailey," said Sue Ellen. "Marcus

was trouble long before you ever arrived. He thinks he should have had Ryder's job, and he's determined to cause trouble for Ryder any way he can."

"And I make it so easy," Hailey murmured. "Look at what happened this past weekend. I don't want to cause anyone more trouble." Especially Ryder, she thought mournfully.

"What about class?" Curtis asked. "I thought maybe you were here because you were going to hold class again."

"I was, but—" She shook her head. "There's no point. I have less than a week to go, anyway."

"What do you mean?" Curtis asked. "I thought you liked it here."

I do. More than I should. "My father invited me to visit him for a month. The month is nearly at an end." She tried for a smile. "I'm not sure the team can afford for me to be here even that long." She gripped the door handle.

"So, you're really leaving?" Sue Ellen asked. "Now? What about your father?"

Hailey's heart clutched. "I'll talk to him, of course."

"Talk to me about what?" Her father appeared in the open doorway.

Hailey froze for a second. She cared about him, she really did. He'd gotten along fine without her for years, though. And he couldn't want the uproar to continue.

Sue Ellen and Curtis suddenly vanished from the room, leaving her alone with her father.

Hailey straightened her shoulders. "I have to leave a little earlier than I'd planned."

"I...see." The warmth she'd grown accustomed to transformed into caution. "May I ask why?"

Among the things she'd learned about this man were that he was noble and giving. If she used not wanting to complicate his life as her reason, he'd dismiss that as a concern.

That didn't change the fact that she was causing problems for all of them. Especially Ryder.

So she stiffened her resolve. "My life is in California. I've been gone too long. I'm going to lose all my students if I don't return right away."

"You have students here," he countered. "You could have more."

Please, Daddy. I'm trying to help you. "North Carolina isn't really right for me." Even if it had come to feel like home.

A fleeting image of Ryder's log cabin was an arrow to her heart.

"What do I tell Brandon?"

Brandon. She'd forgotten all about him. "I don't think he'll be surprised, but I'll make sure there are no repercussions for the team."

"I wasn't thinking about Brandon the sponsor—I was talking about the man."

"There's nothing between us." That much was true. After the fight, Brandon had asked her how long she and Ryder had been involved. She hadn't tried to deny that she'd been unexpectedly drawn to Ryder, however clear it was now that he'd changed his mind. The resulting conversation had been awkward, and she was so afraid that she'd harmed the team, however gracious Brandon had been.

"I'd hoped—" If anything, her father's face closed down more. "I'm sorry things didn't work out, Hailey." Sorrow shadowed his eyes, and Hailey wanted to throw herself into his arms and weep. Give in and stay.

He hesitated, then spoke again. "Sweetheart, is this about our past? We've never discussed it."

"That's over and done," she said hastily. Hadn't she sworn to herself that she'd keep the past where it belonged?

"I need you to know that I'm not proud of how I handled things."

"We really don't need to discuss it." *Please stop before I break down.*

"I think we do, however painful it is for me."

"For you?" she blurted. "But you got along fine without

me for years." For the first time, she let herself really feel how much that had hurt.

"That's completely untrue. I missed you like crazy. I tried again and again to find a way to be with you, but I had to be on the road as I built the team, and your mother would never let you go out of town with me. Every time I begged to keep you for a weekend or a summer vacation, she'd throw roadblocks in my way. I sent you cards and I called, but you never responded, not once. I was working so hard building a future so I could take care of you, but after a while, a man just has to know when to give up."

He paused, but she was too stunned to respond immediately, and he went on. "I convinced myself I was doing what you wanted, what was best for you by letting you go. I made sure I paid the child support on time, and I sent you gifts for birthdays and Christmases, but—" he glanced up at her "—I never knew if you liked any of them."

She frowned. "But I wrote thank-you notes for every single one, and I never got a card or knew about any phone calls."

"Sweetheart, I promise I'm telling you the truth."

"But..." So many scenes from her childhood looked different in this light. How much Hailey was discouraged from making friends, how often she and her mother moved. Her mother had never made friends anywhere they lived, really, and her relationships with men were few.

"You seriously tried to call? You wanted me to visit?"

"More than that, I would have liked for you to live with me. I should never have given her sole custody."

"Surely Mother wouldn't have..." But the only explanation she could see was exactly that, her mother withheld those from her. "What kind of mother robs her child of a father?"

"She was never happy with me, honey, but I swear I tried."

She couldn't take it all in. Her entire life was a lie. "I'm sorry...I don't know what..." If she didn't leave this second, she would fall completely apart. "I have to go."

His face went carefully neutral. "How soon are you leaving?"

"I...I'll check for a flight while I pack."

"No need for that. I'll have the plane take you whenever you're ready."

"That's too expensive for you, and you'll need the plane for Bristol."

"If you're leaving early, the plane will be back in time." His tone softened. "Please, if I can't convince you to stay, at least let me do this for you, sweetheart."

Could she feel any worse? She realized the answer was yes when he asked his next question.

"What about Ryder?"

"Ryder?" she echoed. "Dad, Ryder doesn't even like me. He'll be the happiest to see me go." Her heart ached to be leaving her father, but she had to sort this out, had to get away somewhere she could think. She hugged him quickly. "I'm so sorry, Daddy. None of this is your fault." Then, before she fell apart completely, she scurried out the door.

"She's *WHAT?*" RYDER stared at Sue Ellen.

"Hailey's leaving. She's gone to pack right now."

He should be happy; she would be out of his hair. Life would be simple again.

No, life would be empty, he realized. Heaven help him.

"How did Dixon take it?"

"I wasn't here when she told him," Sue Ellen said. "But he's been sitting in his office, staring at the same piece of paper for an hour."

"I want her back in my life," Dixon had said at the beginning. *"It means a lot to me for her to like this place and what I do."*

"Why's she leaving?" Though he was pretty sure he didn't need to ask.

"Dixon said she doesn't like it here, but—"

"But what?"

"What happened at Michigan, Ryder? It's not like you to lose your cool."

I've done a lot of things that weren't like me since Hailey Rogers showed up. For a second, he indulged in memories of how perfect she'd looked in his shirt, sitting in his grandmother's rocker.

She says she doesn't like it here, he reminded himself. A princess, after all. He snapped to rigid attention. "No point in going over old ground. We've both got work to do." Sue Ellen recoiled at his abrupt dismissal, but his head was already whirling and he had to get it on straight. The team could not take another week of turmoil.

The team was his job.

Hailey Rogers was not.

But even as he strode swiftly to his office, he knew he couldn't give up that easily.

HAILEY WAS PACKING when someone pounded at the front door. She frowned; she wasn't expecting company, and surely if the pilot had moved up the flight, someone would have called her.

The pounding continued.

"Hailey!" yelled a too-familiar voice. "Answer this door. I'm not leaving until you do."

"Go away," she muttered. "I don't want to talk to you, Ryder."

But Ryder couldn't hear her. And he didn't stop pounding. Or yelling loud enough to wake the dead.

"All right!" See what he did to her? She, who never raised her voice, was yelling right back. She stomped her way to the front door and wrenched it open. "Go away!" She shoved the door shut—

Ryder caught it in midswing. "Not until we talk." He stalked past her without an invitation. "You're going to just run away, no matter how it impacts your father? You hurt him. He loves you, Hailey, and he's a good man."

"I know that."

"Then why are you leaving? Are you punishing him?"

"No. I just have to figure out some things."

"Do you have a clue how much that man wants you to like it here? How badly he wants you to be part of his life?"

"He never even told people he had a daughter."

"He explained everything to you, how he thought you didn't want anything to do with him."

"How can you know this?" she challenged.

"Because I did what you should have done a long time ago, *Princess*." His tone was fingernails on a blackboard. "I asked. Your dad made it clear from the start that having you approve of his life was of critical importance, which is why he asked me to make sure you were comfortable here."

Her heart sank. He'd only been trying to please her father? Was everything she thought he'd felt for her a lie, too? How could it not be, when he'd walked away from her so easily? "When did you ask?"

"Right before I drove over here. After I found him in his office, with all the life drained out of him." He stepped toward her. "I owe that man everything. *Everything*. He gave a gawky kid a chance, and he encouraged me every step of the way. I wouldn't be where I am if not for your dad."

"So you did your job, but you aren't in control of my decisions. I have to figure out what to do about all this." She gestured toward her suitcase. "So I'm packing, and I should think you'd be happy."

"What the hell does that mean?"

"You said I was a distraction. That fight was a perfect example. Last week's race was a disaster, and the team can't stand another lousy week."

"So?"

"*So?*" She narrowed her gaze and closed the distance between them, drilling a finger into his chest. "Ever since we made love—had sex, I mean—you've been in a lousy mood. Fine. I get it. It was a mistake. I'm over it. I stayed out of your way, I canceled all my classes and didn't set foot in the shop, but that wasn't enough. The whole team suffered because somehow I violated your precious distance, and you had to make me back up." She held up her hands in surrender. "Okay, fine, you don't want me. I'm backing up, Ryder. All the way to California."

"But—"

"Isn't that what you want of me, to stay out of your way? Isn't that why you couldn't wait to get rid of me after the night…the night we…" she stammered.

"Wait. Me, get rid of you? Babe, you gave me such a cold shoulder I might as well have walked into a deep freeze. And you couldn't wait to spend all your time with Brandon. Where is the rich boy, anyway?"

"You…you…" Her expression was murderous. "Brandon is a very nice man, not that you would know one thing about being nice. And I never gave you the cold shoulder—it was you!" She stabbed a finger into his chest. "You couldn't wait to get away from me. You were embarrassed to be seen with me at Maudie's. You called that night a mistake!"

"Me? You called it a mistake, not me. 'Never do anything so stupid again,'" he quoted. "Recall saying that, Princess?"

"Stop calling me Princess! And get out!" She whirled away, but he caught her before she could leave the room.

As he reeled her back, she ducked her head to hide her tears. "Don't. Don't cry."

"Go away." She brushed at her eyes.

He reached for his lucky grease rag, keeping a grip on her wrist. "Blow your nose," he instructed gently.

"Let me go first."

"Not a chance." Instead, he held the rag for her, then wiped her nose like a child's. He stuffed the rag back in his pocket, then tilted her face up to his, though she stubbornly kept her eyes cast down. "You hurt me, Hailey. When you called that night a mistake." He drew in a deep breath. "It was the most amazing night of my life."

Her gaze flew upward. "Really?"

"Really." He bent his head to hers and brushed a kiss over her lips. "I didn't want to go to the shop. I wanted to stay there forever."

A glimmer of a smile. "Mr. Workaholic?" Her face softened. "Me, too. I love your place."

A warmth filled his chest. "So why did you stay away from me?"

"You're kidding, right? Everyone at Maudie's saw us, and Marcus was sneering and you looked miserable, and I'd promised no more distractions and then you wouldn't talk to me and you treated me like I had the plague—"

He put one finger to her lips to stop the torrent. "Okay, besides that, I mean." He began to smile, and her heart gave a little flip.

"I don't know what to do about you, Ryder."

"I'm a little baffled myself, honey. I…I can't remember the last time I had a date, much less lost my mind over a woman."

"Really?"

"Really. So isn't there something you want to tell me, Hailey?"

"Me? Like what?"

"Like that you're crazy about me or you at least want me to kiss you again or maybe even that you—" He swallowed hard. "That you might love me."

"Love you?" she echoed.

"Never mind." He let her go and turned around.

"No!" She skirted around and planted herself in his path. "Ryder, how can you expect me to say something like that?"

"I said never mind." He took a step to the side.

"Not so fast, mister." She grasped his hand. "I didn't mean that I couldn't, or wouldn't, just…why me first?"

A slow, teasing grin. "Because you're the girl."

She goggled. "What?"

He shrugged. "Women say that stuff easier." Her mouth dropped open, and his expression was pure mischief. "It's harder for guys."

If she could have incinerated him with a look, she would have. "You Neanderthal. You baboon, you—"

He started laughing. "My, oh, my, Miss Hailey. Granola Girl does have a temper, didn't I tell you?"

As Hailey spluttered, he drew her against him, picked her up and twirled her around.

"Put me down, you throwback, you—"

He came to a halt and stopped her outburst with a kiss that quickly turned so scorching hot they both moaned.

"I love you, Hailey Rogers," he said against her lips. "You drive me absolutely insane, but for some perverse reason, I seem to find that more fun than I've had in all my years."

She melted against him. "Oh, Ryder…" She stood on tiptoe and gave him a kiss he would never forget. When she came up for air then started working at his buttons while she went back for seconds, he put his hand between their mouths.

"Uh-uh, sweet pea. You don't steal my virtue without saying it back."

"Saying what?"

"Hailey…"

She smiled at him from the heart. Then she threw her arms around his neck and laughed out loud. "I love you, Ryder McGraw, you insane, aggravating, control freak of a man. Now help me shove that suitcase off my bed and make love to me."

"Now?"

Just then they heard the front door open. "Hailey? Honey, we need to talk."

Ryder froze at the sound of his employer's voice.

Hailey's eyes went wide. "Daddy?"

They both heard Dixon's footfall on the stairs.

"Stay here," she whispered, and scooted from the room before he could react.

"DADDY, WHAT ARE YOU doing here?" She cut a glance toward her room, then hurried down the stairs to the center landing to forestall him.

"I can't let you go."

She blinked. "What?"

"I gave you up once for what I thought was your own good, but it was wrong for both of us. I missed too much of your life." His eyes were dark and haunted.

She bit her lip. "I thought you didn't want me. I didn't understand why, and it hurt so badly."

He scaled the stairs between them, and suddenly she was in his arms. "Of course I wanted you. Oh, sweetheart, if I'd known…" He shook his head and clasped her more tightly. "I couldn't give you all my attention during a race weekend, so I…" He leaned back. "I gave up too easily," he repeated. "As I've never given up on anything else in my life." He gripped her shoulders. "But I'm not doing that this time. I want you in my life, and not just for an occasional visit. Please don't go."

"But—"

"I don't want her to leave, either, Dixon." Ryder emerged from her room.

Hailey tensed. "Ryder…"

"I love your daughter, sir. I want to marry her."

Her father's eyes went as wide as her own had.

And all she'd heard was the *I love you* part. "Marry you?" she echoed.

Her father's gaze shifted to her. "Is that what you want, sweetheart?"

She stared at Ryder, whose eyes were locked on hers. "It's the first I've heard of this. When were you going to tell me? Or were you just going to bark an order, Mr. Crew Chief?"

He grinned. "Since you listen to me so well?" He crossed the landing. "You said you love my cabin. I love having you in it. What do you say, Hailey? Will you marry me?"

She felt her father's arm tense where it rested around her

shoulders. "And live here? In North Carolina? What would I do?"

"Travel with me—er, with us, sir." He shifted his gaze back to her. "Teach yoga. Or I'll give you a job. Want Greg's job?"

"You can't give me Greg's job!"

"Yes, he can," said her father.

"Greg hasn't done anything wrong," she protested.

Ryder's eyebrows rose. "That's not what you've been saying since the day you arrived."

"But I'm a distraction, you said so. And Jeb had a terrible race last week."

Ryder started down the stairs. "That was my fault because you messed me up so much. He'll have a better one this week."

"But I, uh, I—"

"What is it, sweetheart?" her father asked. "What's wrong?"

She backed away from both of them. "I can't get married."

Ryder slipped past her father and stood very close to her. "You told me you love me." Green eyes turned dark and intense.

"Sweetheart, is it because of us? Your mother and me?"

"No—yes. I don't know. I just—" Hailey bit her lip. *What is wrong with me?* Then she heard her mother's voice in her head, snippets from years and years of misery her mother had brought on herself.

She shook her head to stop the playback. "I'm not my mother," she said to Ryder.

"No," he said cautiously.

"And racing wasn't the problem." She looked at her father.

"We were never well-suited, honey. If I'd been an accountant, we wouldn't have meshed well, either. And it's not all her fault."

"Lots of families in the sport manage," Ryder had said. *"Some of them home-school and others travel part-time."*

"You work too much," she said to Ryder.

"I know." He sighed. "Part of it's the job, but most of it's me." He smiled and moved closer. "I didn't have any reason not to before."

"But what about the team? You okay with this, Daddy? If Ryder eases up?"

"I've told him myself more than a few times that he'll burn out if he doesn't slow down. I'd like to keep him around for a long time."

"Maybe you could teach me yoga."

Her gaze snapped to Ryder's. "Are you serious?"

"No." He grinned. "Well…maybe. But you can sure teach others. Even—" he exhaled deeply "—my pit crew. I've seen the results of your influence."

"Really?" She hesitated. "Is that a bribe, Mr. McGraw?"

"Would it work?" He took her in his arms and bent his head to her, brushing her mouth with his own.

Her father cleared his throat. "Uh, I'll just…I'm going back to work."

Hailey tried to pull away, but Ryder wasn't letting her go anywhere. "Goodbye, sir." Dismissal was clear in his tone.

"Ryder!" she said, scandalized.

But her father was already down the stairs.

Hailey looked at Ryder.

Ryder stared at Hailey. "Will you?"

"Teach you yoga? Sure," she teased.

He shook his head. "Marry me."

Suddenly, from downstairs, they heard her father again. "Ryder? Son—"

"Uh-oh. This is where he fires me for messing with his daughter," Ryder whispered.

"Take the day off," her father said. "As long as you don't let her leave."

Hailey giggled. Ryder started in surprise. "Um, thank you, sir."

The front door closed, and they heard the lock turn loudly.

"You heard the man," Ryder said.

"You can't really afford to take the day off, can you?"

"Not really."

"Bristol's a big race," she said as her heart sank.

"It is."

"The team needs a better week."

"Yep."

She stepped back from him. "Go ahead and go. I understand."

His eyes were sparkling with mischief, and he was shaking his head. "So you're not going to give me a reason to stay? Help me learn to slow down?" He stalked her as she backed toward her bedroom. "What kind of yoga teacher are you? Maybe you should teach me that relaxation stuff," he said as he closed in on her. "Though I don't feel much like relaxing right now." His lips began to cruise down her throat. "Truth is, I'm afraid if you don't do something quick, I just might find myself back at the shop. Help me, Teach." His tone was playful as he caressed her while his teeth nipped lightly at her ear lobe. "You have to save me."

Hailey giggled. Sighed. Couldn't help moaning just a little.

"Stay," she murmured. "I'll stay, too."

His head rose. "You mean it? With me?"

Hailey looked at him and thought about how she'd always been so careful not to get too involved. How much she'd let fear rule her for too long.

"My father loves me," she said. "You love me."

"I do. He does. Will you stay, Hailey? Make your life with me? Give him that second chance, too?"

Hailey swallowed hard, then realized how free she suddenly felt. "I will." Then she laughed for pure joy. Opened her arms wide.

And grabbed on tight to the dream she'd thought for so long could never be hers.

* * * * *

Shifting Gears

Peggy Webb

For Debra Webb, dear friend and fellow writer.
Long live the Twisted Sisters!

CHAPTER ONE

THE DAY STARTED LIKE any other Tuesday, except that Rue Larrabee woke thirty minutes later than she usually did with the uneasy feeling that she'd not only overslept, but that she'd also somehow spent her entire life missing the boat.

Shaking off the feeling, she leaped out of bed and grabbed her clothes. She wasn't about to scrimp on dolling herself up.

Beauty was her business, and by George, she intended to flaunt every one of her natural charms—a thick tangle of red hair, pouty lips she painted cherry-red, a generous figure she was partial to showing off with low-cut blouses and slim, well-fitted Audrey Hepburn ankle pants.

Today she chose a blouse in a festive golden shade, the color of the chrysanthemums she'd bought in pots last week hoping to beat the summer heat and usher in fall. She topped her ensemble with a pair of sensible espadrilles and dangling earrings as big as Arkansas, then grabbed her purse and headed to Maudie's to pick up the box of doughnuts she always bought for the girls at Cut 'N' Chat. Rue was sole proprietor of the best little beauty shop in Mooresville, North Carolina, and she was happy to say she owned it lock, stock and curling irons.

As she went downstairs, she whipped out her cell phone and called Daisy Brookshire, her most reliable hair stylist.

"I'm running late, sweetie."

"Good grief, Rue. Is the world coming to an end?"

"Possibly. Can you hold down the fort?"

"I'm feeling so good I could tame tigers. Can you pick up some extra cream-filled doughnuts for me? I could eat a house." Daisy, pregnant and big as a barrel, was eating for two.

"Will do. See you in a bit."

Rue's little two-story cottage was only three streets over from her shop, which was right next door to Maudie's Down Home Diner. Today was gorgeous, and Rue walked, as she usually did in beautiful weather.

She had only gone half a block when somebody whistled at her. Though it was only that cute young NASCAR hunk, Bart Branch, driving his silver sports car with the top down, Rue's spirits perked up.

While she could be the poster child for Women Who Choose Bad Boyfriends, she had no intention of acting like the most often jilted woman in town.

Grinning, she hollered, "Pick on somebody your own age, Bart."

As he waved and tooted his horn, then disappeared around the corner, Rue wondered why she had never had the good fortune to pick somebody like Bart. He was one of the nicest men she knew, in spite of having Hilton Branch for a father.

Though her bad luck paled compared to the Branch family's misfortune over Hilton's imprisonment for shady financial dealings, Rue still wondered if maybe her unlucky encounters with men had to do with her approach. If she'd used her ears and eyes instead of her big heart, she'd never have gone out with the string of men who dumped her, starting with her date at senior prom—who took a shine to cheerleader Barbie and a powder at the same time—and ending with Mark Hayworth, that wart on a hog who left her at the altar. With one of Rue's bridesmaids, for crying out loud. That heifer!

There was no sense dwelling on it. At forty-four Rue had long ago given up on men and turned her attention to better things. Like taking care of everybody with a sob story who wandered into her beauty shop.

The Statue of Liberty of Cut 'N' Chat. That was Rue. Give her the tired, the poor, the wretched masses yearning for a better life, and she'd fix them up with hot soup, a place to stay and the good advice she wished somebody had given her when she was twenty years younger.

Too late now. Her parents had died in a car crash when Rue was eighteen, and even if she'd wanted her older sister to fit the bill, Janice was too busy trying to get out of Mooresville to bother with a sister ten years younger. She still didn't have time for Rue. She was too busy chasing down the world's most exotic places for her travel magazine to bother with anything that looked like *family*.

Rue, on the other hand, adored her hometown. When Maudie's came into view, she picked up her pace. The diner would be filled with people she knew and loved—NASCAR teams and the locals who viewed her as a beloved icon, the woman who could make them laugh and make them look good at the same time.

Rue pushed open the door, smiling. Everybody from Sheila Trueblood, the diner's owner, to Al Jordan, the cook, called out a greeting.

"Looking good, Rue," Al said. "If I didn't already have Louise, I'd be knocking on your door."

"Al, I'm going to marry the first man I find who can make biscuits like yours."

"I'll dance at that wedding," Sheila said. Whipcord thin and a virtual dynamo, she brought the energy of youth into everything she did, including packing up Rue's usual doughnut order—with a few extras for Daisy.

Everybody in the diner jumped on Sheila's remark and joined in the fun. At least two NASCAR drivers promised to give Rue away and one, Jeb Stallworth, who had a formidable record of ending his races in Victory Lane, even promised to lend his cabin in Denver as the honeymoon getaway.

For a moment, it seemed that a wedding for Rue was just around the corner, and she got flushed thinking of the possibilities. In her excitement, Rue forgot to fasten her change purse. Quarters, nickels, dimes and pennies cascaded to the floor and willfully scattered themselves every which way.

Not the least embarrassed, Rue dropped on all fours to gather her runaway change. She'd survived far worse things than this.

Rue wasn't alone for long. Before she had retrieved two quarters, she found herself crawling around on the floor with Mooresville's pediatrician, the town's postman and five NASCAR drivers. All intent on helping and all of them laughing.

Sheila put on a fresh pot of coffee, then planted her arms on her hips in mock horror. "Rue Larrabee, you're having so much fun down there I'm about to wonder what you're up to."

"There's nothing like a good romp on the floor to start the day right."

Amid howls of laughter, Rue crawled after a particularly elusive quarter. She was within reaching distance when it vanished under a pair of well-worn but polished ostrich-skin boots. Size twelve, judging from the looks of them.

Rue's gaze followed the boots upward to a pair of long, blue-jean-clad legs, a belt with the NASCAR logo, a soft denim shirt open at the collar over a delicious-looking chest. Next came a chiseled chin, beautifully molded lips and cool blue-gray eyes.

Rue almost lost her pizzazz. She was practically groveling at the feet of Andrew Clark, six gorgeous feet of careful reserve. If ever there was a man who wore a Keep Out sign, it was the owner of FastMax Racing.

After he pulled off a stunning coup last year—his stepson Garrett had won the NASCAR Sprint Cup Series championship, the first time in seventeen years a one-car garage had done such a thing—Andrew had gone from underdog to a man well on his way to NASCAR royalty, especially if Garrett kept ending up in Victory Lane.

While Rue regularly kidded around with NASCAR drivers in Maudie's, there was something both mesmerizing and intimidating about this team owner. Too handsome for his own good, he was just the kind who might make her forget her bad relationship history and lose her head.

She'd always kept herself at a safe distance from him, and for whatever his reasons, he'd certainly never approached her. And now she was literally at his feet.

You could have knocked her over with a foam hair roller when Andrew knelt and scooped up her quarter. "Is this what you're looking for?"

Oh, even worse. Now she was practically nose-to-nose with him, their delicate balance of silence shattered. If he'd been grinning, Rue could have laughed it off, but there was not a hint that Andrew found their situation even remotely amusing.

To her heightened senses, it seemed that all noise in the diner had ceased, that everybody had abandoned biscuits and country ham in order to hear what the unflappable Rue would say to the unattainable Andrew Clark.

"Andrew, I do believe you have what every woman is looking for."

Oh, help. Had she just said that? Regretting her penchant for saying the first thing that popped into her mind, unsettled by the intense scrutiny of cool silvery eyes and the flush that completely overtook her, Rue snatched the quarter, stood up, grabbed her doughnuts and shot out of the shop.

She was no sooner out of the diner than she realized she'd

left her purse behind. Wild horses couldn't drag her back in there. Andrew Clark probably thought she was the worst-behaved woman in town.

Crawling around on the floor in a public place was bad enough if you were eighteen and skinny as a toothpick. But when you're over forty and working hard to keep your back-side from attaining the shape and size of your over-stuffed recliner, you have no business advertising the fact at Maudie's Down Home Diner.

Sheila would send somebody over to the shop with Rue's purse. The best thing she could do was forget about the incident and start her day over. Start it off right.

Besides, Rue had better things to do than worry over a divorced man who wouldn't know the meaning of fun if it grabbed him by the seat of his pants. Everybody in town—including NASCAR heroes—flocked to her shop for great cuts and large doses of fun. But Andrew Clark never darkened her door.

So be it. She would color him *gone*.

Her shop bell tinkled when she pushed open the door. Rue marched in with a big smile on her face. She loved the smell of green-apple shampoo and floral hair spray and sassy nail polish. She loved the cozy feeling of women with towels wrapped around their wet hair sharing the town's stories as they flipped through magazines that told the latest doings of their favorite movie stars.

She was glad to see that Daisy had already shampooed Rue's first customer and good friend, Patsy Clark Grosso. Grace Clark was also waiting her turn at the wash basin. She was an extraordinarily successful caterer as well as the daughter who'd been stolen from Patsy and her husband as a baby and only discovered last year in a fairy-tale ending.

Careful, Rue told herself. *No jokes about falling at the feet of Andrew Clark.*

Patsy was Andrew's sister. And Grace Clark was Andrew's niece as well as his stepdaughter-in-law. She was the one who had finally captured the heart of Andrew's sinfully good-looking and former playboy stepson, race car driver, Garrett Clark.

Placing the doughnuts on a table in the middle of the shop, Rue announced, "Chow time."

Daisy was first to the table. Poor little thing. She was trying to save up for the baby she would raise alone, stuffing every penny she could make in the drawer of her styling station. If Rue could wave a magic wand, she'd replace the baby's father, who had died. But short of miracles, she was doing the next best thing: planning a shower for Daisy.

Grace and Patsy, holding a towel on her head, grabbed a doughnut. They chatted about next week's race at Indianapolis and speculated about which drivers would be auctioned at the upcoming NASCAR charity benefit. Rue thought it was wonderful how quickly this mother and daughter had bonded after being separated for more than thirty years.

The shop bell tinkled and in walked Bart Branch.

"Save any doughnuts for me?"

"You're early, Bart," Rue said, as if she had to ask why. Every time he got his curly blond hair trimmed, he came early to kid with the women. Bart loved to keep a good joke going.

"Somebody has to keep you out of trouble, Rue."

"I can't imagine what you're talking about."

"The caper at Maudie's. Big news travels fast in a small town."

Rue hoped that big news didn't include details of what she'd said to Andrew Clark. She still blushed to think of it. And she wasn't even the blushing kind.

She was trying to think of a comeback quip when the shop's bell jangled again. At the rate people were pouring into her shop, Rue was going to have to send Daisy for another box of doughnuts.

Before Rue turned around to greet the newcomer, she saw Bart go from devil-may-care to Little Boy Falling in Love with the Cutest Pet in the Shop Window.

"Rue, I brought the purse you left in the diner."

The soft voice belonged to Mellie Donovan, the new waitress from Maudie's Diner. With her big brown doe eyes and wispy hair, she looked as fragile as a baby bird. Every time Rue saw her, she wanted to wrap her in warm blankets and sing "Rescue the Perishing," though everybody in town knew Rue couldn't carry a tune in a bucket. As it was, she hugged Mellie and thanked her profusely for returning the purse.

"Have a doughnut, Mellie." Rue thought the young woman could use a little meat on her bones.

"I have to hurry back."

"I'd be glad to escort you." Bart had mostly recovered, but he still looked a little starstruck. Everybody in the shop knew he'd been making eyes at Mellie.

"Oh." Mellie's hands fluttered to her spiky, dark hair as if she were checking to see if it was still there. "Thank you, but no. I don't need anybody."

Everybody needs somebody, Rue thought. *Except me.*

When Mellie waved at Daisy then left the shop, the usually cheerful Bart sounded downright crestfallen.

"I guess I lucked out again."

Rue winked at him. "I'm older than God but you've still got me."

"Rue Larrabee," Bart said, "the woman who founded the Tuesday Tarts will never be old."

When he grabbed her in a dance hold and twirled her around, everybody in the shop clapped.

Rue was doing what she did best, making other people happy. And that felt good.

Still, the uneasy feeling she'd awakened with persisted, that she'd lived her life vicariously, that while she was rescuing everybody else, her boat had sailed away.

Rue grabbed a hair dryer and a styling brush and went to work on Patsy's hair. There was nothing like work to stave off the blues.

CHAPTER TWO

ANDREW CLARK'S GARAGE was a beehive of activity as they geared up for the race at Indianapolis. A team of analysts was going over race data on a bank of computer screens. Hydraulics screamed, metal tools clanked and blowtorches shot sharp blue light as mechanics bustled around various race car parts. Jared Hunt, owner of Jared Hunt Engines, Inc., and touted by the press as a miracle worker and engine whisperer, put the engine of Garrett's much vaunted No. 402 car through diagnostics.

Billy Cook, marketing director, was sequestered in his office down the hall planning what Andrew considered a brilliant marketing strategy, while Andrew was holed up with his crew chief, Robbie, his spotter, Jamie, and Garrett doing a postmortem on the race in Chicago.

Though Andrew would have preferred to be in his more austere and businesslike office, his stepson felt more comfortable in his office among his rather brilliant nature photographs and his motley collection of memorabilia, which included a plastic figure of the Tasmanian Devil. Andrew swelled with pride. This was the stepson who had chosen to live with him instead of his own flighty mother, the son he'd brought up alone, the son who had saved Andrew and the entire FastMax team from financial ruin by winning last year's NASCAR Sprint Cup championship.

There was a knock on the door followed by the appearance

of a beautiful, blue-eyed blonde with the smile as well as the heart of an angel.

"Surprise!" Grace said. Garrett bounded to the door to kiss his wife, while Andrew pulled out a chair for his stepdaughter-in-law. He adored her. She not only loved his son, but she had also given Garrett a ready-made family— three precious children—and provided him a stability his mother never had.

A woman's touch. Even Andrew, for all his love and attention, had been unable to give that to his stepson.

"Did you bring something good to nibble on?" Garrett said, and everybody grinned. Grace owned Gourmet by Grace, had her own TV cooking show and had penned a NASCAR cookbook.

"You mean, besides me," she teased her husband, and then took a black-and-white checkered cloth off a basket of steaming brownies.

The crew chief was the first to dive in. "Better watch out, boy. I'm gonna steal her from you." The idea of Robbie, the approximate size and shape of a fireplug with the pugnacious personality of a bulldog, stealing Grace brought howls of laugher.

While the men vied for a spot at the brownie basket, Grace said to Andrew, "Buying that antique race car was a brilliant idea. It seems meant for you."

She was referring to Andrew's newly acquired 1946 Novi. With a supercharged, 4-Cam, V-8 engine, the historic Novi had set records at Indy and at Bonneville Salt Flats. The Novi and the people involved in its development were part of the Indianapolis legend. That Andrew had one of the only two ever built was a great source of pride. The other was in the Speedway Museum at Indy.

"First a bribe and now flattery," he teased. "What are you up to, Grace?"

"Do I have to be up to something to visit you?"

"Probably."

Grace put on a pretty pout, and Andrew saw how his step-son had fallen for this lovely and charming woman. Garrett had chosen wisely and well. Andrew wished he might have had the same good luck with women, but the moment passed quickly. He had too much to do to waste time in regrets. Last year he'd taken enormous financial risks, mortgaging and leveraging everything he had, to get Garrett to the champion-ship. But winning the NASCAR Sprint Cup championship was just the beginning of his hard work. Andrew had no inten-tion of letting FastMax and his stepson become a one-shot wonder.

"Since you're going to be an old bear, I might as well just spit it out. I want you to be part of the 'date with a bachelor' auction."

"I've already told you I can't, Grace." Andrew hated telling her no, but on some things he had to draw the line.

"Aw, come on, Dad. Pamper my sweet little wife."

Grace playfully tweaked Garrett's ear. "Your *sweet little wife* can handle herself, darling." To Andrew she said, "That's why I'm asking again. You can't say *no*."

"Why not?"

"For one thing, you've always supported the NASCAR children's charities."

"Yes. With a check."

"For another, the benefit is the brainchild of none other than Patsy Clark Grosso. There's no way you can turn her down."

"My sister doesn't scare me." In fact, he and his sister had patched their differences over Garrett's win last year and now talked nearly every day. The balancing act was to be competitors and still be family. Having three grandchildren in common helped. "My answer is still no."

"What else do you have to do Wednesday night?"

"Yeah, Dad. Everything's under control here. You need to loosen up."

Grace and Garrett thought they had a good point, but Andrew didn't see it that way. He had more than enough to fill his life—Garrett and now Grace and the kids. He had FastMax and his cars, plus the adrenaline-rush excitement and bone-deep contentment of NASCAR. Though Andrew had never been a shining star, Garret's win had catapulted them into the limelight. Everybody, the press included, loved a great "underdog takes the title" story.

Additionally, he had his books, his gardens and his late-night classic Western movies. What more could a man want?

Though he had no social life outside of his immediate family by choice, Andrew figured his daughter-in-law must think him the most boring man on earth. Still, there was no way he could get up in public and be auctioned off to a woman who was bound to have an agenda. They always did.

Besides, he was out of his league around women. As if his failed marriage to Garret's mom wasn't enough to prove that, look at his track record prior to marriage. Women flocked to him, all right, but only to try to change him into something he was not—some kind of giddy, good-time Charlie, all fun and games.

Take this morning, for instance. Any other man trapped at Maudie's with that flamboyant beauty-shop owner practically upended at his feet would have rescued the embarrassing situation with a clever remark. Andrew had stood there like somebody in a shootout at the OK Corral.

Heck, you could look under the hood of a car and figure out everything you needed to know. But women didn't have hoods, and even if they did and you could look under there, you'd see such a tangled mess of jumbled-up baggage, you wouldn't know which way was out.

"I'm sorry, Grace. I can't help you out."

"Can't or won't?" she said, and Garrett gave her a high-five.

"You two are conspiring against me."

"Kick up your heels, Dad."

"Son, you'd better be concentrating on your next race instead of urging an old dog to try new tricks."

"The auction will only take a few hours of your time," Grace said. "Won't you do it for me? Please."

Though he knew Grace was using emotional blackmail, Andrew felt like a cad telling her *absolutely not*.

"All right, then."

"Way to go, Dad." Garrett winked, while Robbie and Jamie looked like they were holding back big guffaws.

"That's fabulous! Thank you." She threw her arms around his neck and hugged him. Grace's joy seemed all out of proportion to her request. Andrew figured he'd just been cornered into something he was going to live to regret.

"What do I have to do?"

"Nothing. Just show up at the auction, take the woman who bids for you to dinner, say good-night and go home."

That all sounded too easy. Andrew had the sinking-gut feeling of a man who had just jumped out of an airplane without a parachute.

RUE HAD FOUNDED THE Tuesday Tarts with the idea that women needed regular sessions with friends in order to remain sane. The Tuesday Tarts had no dues, no agenda and no rules except one: don't take yourself too seriously. Because the membership was made up of women, such as Patsy and Grace, who were involved in NASCAR racing as wives and relatives of drivers or team owners, there were no attendance requirements.

Their meeting location was always at Maudie's. Besides catching up, they managed to get a lot of things done. Last year they'd raised enough money at a one-day carnival on the street in front of the Cut 'N' Chat and Maudie's Down Home Diner to add two new computers to the Mooresville Public Library.

That evening the talk was about how much money they were going to help raise for the upcoming NASCAR children's charities. Rue was relieved that nobody had mentioned her unfortunate early morning encounter with Andrew Clark.

Suddenly Patsy turned to Rue. "Are you planning to attend the bachelor auction tomorrow night?"

Until today, Rue had actually been thinking about attending. After making a fool of herself in front of Andrew Clark, there was no way she'd attend any event where the odds of seeing him were about one hundred percent.

"Are you kidding? Much as I love my NASCAR drivers and their families, I'm up to my neck with other plans."

"What other plans, Rue?" Patsy asked. Anybody else might have taken her question as nosy, but Rue knew better. Patsy was constantly urging her to look after herself and have some fun instead of trying to take care of everybody in town.

"For one thing, planning Daisy's baby shower."

"We'll have it at the diner." Sheila spoke with the authority of the *last word,* and all the women gathered around to throw in their two cents worth about the baby shower.

Rue's conscience twigged her, but only a bit. She'd only told a small white lie. Shoot, she could plan that shower with her eyes shut.

The only real plans she had for Wednesday night were to shampoo her hair and touch up her roots. Still, she could easily find other things to do. For one thing, she could bake a peach pie for her next-door neighbor, old Mr. Crumpett, whose arthritis was acting up. For another, she could call Mellie and volunteer to babysit her darling little daughter, Lily. She knew Mellie sometimes worked the two-to-ten shift on Wednesday nights, and she often filled in to give the regular sitter, Booie, a break.

The more Rue thought about it, the more she liked that plan. She shouldered her bag and turned to tell everybody good-night, but they were so busy in their huddle, they didn't even notice her.

"Hey, Sheila," Rue yelled. "What's everybody in such a tizzy about?"

"We're discussing punch and cookies for the baby shower." Rue started to put her purse down, but Sheila waved her off. "Go on home and put your feet up. I can handle this."

Rue was more than happy to oblige. It had been a long and eventful day. All she wanted to do was go home, make a cup of tea with vanilla and cream and forget that she had presented her worst side to Andrew Clark at Maudie's Diner.

WEDNESDAY MORNING Rue couldn't bear the thought of stopping by Maudie's. What if she ran in to Andrew Clark? What in the world would she say? *I was just kidding. You don't have what every woman wants.*

Good grief. Why did she think she had to fill every silence with a quip? What was she, town comedienne?

Sighing, she picked up the phone with the full intention of calling Daisy to say, "Sweetie, can you run by Maudie's and pick up the doughnuts this morning?"

Suddenly Rue balked. Why should she change her lifestyle for any man? Besides, Daisy had enough on her mind with plans for raising a baby alone while Rue had an easy day ahead, a short morning's work followed by a long-awaited and much-deserved afternoon off.

Too, if she asked Daisy to pick up doughnuts, she would start asking questions Rue wasn't willing to answer.

Though practically everybody in town flocked to Rue with their secrets, she made a habit of never sharing her personal life. It was easier that way. Less painful. Why dredge up broken dreams? She had her house, her shop, her friends, her gardens. What more could she want?

Rue selected a blouse the color of the cardinal on her front porch railing. It perked her up. Not many redheads had the audacity to wear red. Feeling sassy and almost her old self, Rue grabbed her purse and pranced out of her house.

A MAN OF HABIT, Andrew always had breakfast at Maudie's when he was in town, the same every morning, two eggs sunny-side up with country-fried ham. But on Wednesday he broke his routine and poured himself a bowl of cold cereal with two percent milk. It looked totally unappetizing. And his coffee wouldn't be nearly as good as Sheila's down at the diner.

But what would he say if he saw Rue? Why put both of them in a position to relive an embarrassing moment? Though truth to tell, except for their encounter over the quarter, he only saw her rarely—usually rushing in for her standing doughnut order saying, "I'm late, I'm late." Still, even in passing, she was a woman you'd notice—flamboyant, personable, oozing the kind of charm that could make you forget your own bad experiences with women.

Andrew added bananas to his cereal, but they were over-ripe and he found himself longing for a big plate of ham and eggs. He gazed at his cold breakfast a moment, then dumped it down the drain. He'd never been the kind of man to back down from a challenge, and today that included another possible encounter with that wild yet strangely appealing Rue

Larrabee. Andrew turned on the garbage disposal, watched his ill-fated breakfast vanish and then set out to Maudie's.

The first person he spotted through the plate glass window was Rue. All that red hair. All that charm. Who could miss her?

He wished he could think of something to say besides *good morning,* something clever and witty. But how could a no-nonsense man like Andrew hope to shift gears and transform himself into somebody glib or, at the very least, passably sociable?

Especially around a woman like Rue. She had a public personality so filled with confidence she needed to do nothing more than spill her quarters to have every man in town groveling at her feet. Today she had two NASCAR drivers standing beside her booth, hanging on her every word.

What was she doing eating breakfast, anyway? She usually just popped in for doughnuts.

Sheila spotted him in the doorway and came over. "Your usual table, Andrew?"

"Not today. I'm in a rush. Just fix my usual breakfast to go?"

"Sure thing. We'll have it up in a sec."

A sec wasn't entirely accurate. The diners began to leave their tables and push past him to get to the cash register. No fancy waiters with discreet black leather folders for your credit card at Maudie's. Any minute now, Rue was going to leave her table and he'd be trapped.

No sooner was the thought out than the flashy redhead strolled past him. No, *strolled* was too tame a word. In that red blouse she sashayed, she shimmied. To Andrew's alarmed point of view, she did everything but brush against him and say, "Come up and see me sometime." Which exactly proved his point. He was so out-of-touch with the dating scene he couldn't even think what women might say without quoting

Mae West, an old movie star nobody would know except a man whose rare evenings at home were spent alone, watching reruns.

Actually, what Rue said when she brushed past him was "Pardon me."

"I thought you'd be on the floor in another chase for quarters."

She shot him a withering look. Good lord, what had he said wrong?

"No, usually I'm upright like everybody else. I just get on the floor for fun." She paid for her breakfast then whizzed out the door.

As he watched her exit, he was eternally grateful he didn't have to deal with her, or anybody even remotely like her, on a daily basis. Still, she was appealing in an odd way, and her rebuff stung a bit.

Andrew didn't just thrive on challenge, he thrived on winning. There was no glimmer of victory in his morning's encounter with Rue.

"Here's your order, Andrew...Andrew?"

He came out of a fog. How long had Sheila been standing there? He started to sit down to eat in the diner. He loved the homey feel, the easy camaraderie as townsfolk drifted in and out, Al calling up the orders.

But Andrew had too much work to enjoy a leisurely breakfast. He took his box, paid and drove toward his shop. It was a tornado of noise and motion, Robbie barking orders, the well-choreographed, highly focused team moving about, the wall-hung, flat screen TV blaring. The frantic pace of his racing world would take Andrew's mind off Rue Larrabee.

Still, as he hurried into his office, he wondered if there was a course specifically designed to teach a man how to act around a wildly unsettling woman.

CHAPTER THREE

ON RUE'S RARE Wednesday afternoon at home, she was multitasking, nibbling a ham sandwich for lunch while she was up to her elbows in chocolate chip cookie dough, when the phone rang. It was Patsy.

"Rue, I'm calling to invite you to accompany Dean and me on our private plane to the race at Watkins Glen."

"Oh, my gosh, Patsy." Rue had never been in a private plane. Furthermore, she'd been so busy establishing Cut 'N' Chat, then later keeping up with the enormous volume of customers, she'd never been to an out-of-town NASCAR race. Still, she had too many responsibilities to take off for a NASCAR holiday. "That's wonderful of you, but I just can't."

"I'd thought I'd ask you early to give you time to get all your excuses out of the way before you say *yes*."

Rue could think of several excuses, and every one of them had to do with Patsy's brother. He'd definitely be at the races to cheer Garrett on, and Rue definitely did not want to be within three city blocks of him. Every time she was around that man, she felt like a flustered sixteen-year-old.

"I really can't take time away from the shop." Patsy's blistering silence said she wasn't buying that. "With Daisy being pregnant I can't possibly leave." Rue nearly scorched in the flaming silence following that silly remark. Every one of the Tuesday Tarts knew Daisy's due date was early September.

"I won't take no for an answer, Rue."

"Why don't I just think about it and let you know in a few days?"

"If you don't say yes right this minute, I'm going to go over to the Cut 'N' Chat and personally black out everything on your to-do calendar. I'll bet not a single thing there has anything to do with Rue Larrabee having some fun for herself. Am I right?"

"You're always right, Patsy."

"If I didn't love you, I'd take exception."

Both women laughed. They'd been friends long enough that they could safely tell each other the uncomfortable truth.

"Come on, Rue. I've asked you year after year. Say yes this time. You know I'm going to badger you till you do. I've been patient long enough."

"All right. Yes."

"Good. And believe me, I'm not going to let you change your mind."

Rue went back to her cookie dough with the uneasy feeling that she'd just signed on for more than the race at Watkins Glen.

Rue put the last of the cookies on to bake. Mellie had accepted Rue's offer to babysit Lily this evening, saying Booie would be glad for the break. She wanted everything ready when the toddler got there.

Rue probably would have baked the cookies anyhow. She loved a kitchen that smelled like sugar and butter and chocolate chips.

She also loved gardening. Her favorite activity was puttering around in the garden center. Though she usually went in the evening when most folks were out having dinner with a spouse or a date so she could have the place mostly to herself, she looked forward to being there on a sunny day, rubbing elbows with other people who shared her love of gardening.

With the last of the cookies cooling in the kitchen, Rue

struck out to Patches Garden Center in her old gray sweats, jogging shoes and a pink baseball cap she'd received for a breast cancer awareness run.

At Patches, she went straight to the bulbs. This time every year, she stocked up. She loved burying daffodils in little holes where they would lie underground all winter, undergoing a mysterious transformation that resulted in an explosion of blooms in the spring.

She was thrilled to see that this year Patches had King Alfred bulbs in white with orange centers. The ruffled variety. Feeling like a little kid at Christmas, Rue started piling little bags of bulbs into her shopping cart.

"I understood the rosemary was half price."

Holding a King Alfred in midair, Rue froze. She'd know that voice anywhere. It was Andrew Clark, the next aisle over in the culinary herb section, looking like the man of every woman's dreams.

Ordinarily, Rue would have sashayed over, made some light remark and then gone on about her business. Instead she found herself behind the King Alfreds, staring in secret as if he were a mouthful of forbidden fruit and she was the hungriest woman in town. Good grief, what was the matter with her? It wasn't as if she was a daffodil bulb set to germinate and blossom. Who wanted to blossom with a man, anyhow? After six or eight attempts, followed by six or eight failures, why even try? Besides, she was so old she was about to get root rot.

Rue scooped her bulbs out of the basket and hurried off to pay. For goodness sake, it wasn't as if she'd never seen Andrew in Patches. Last Christmas he'd been going out with an orchid as she came in. And once or twice she'd seen him pondering over the potting soil. She'd just never seen him after she'd been crawling around on the floor at his feet, sporting a side that was definitely not her best.

Hurrying out, Rue didn't breathe normally till she was in the parking lot behind the wheel of her ancient Mustang convertible. Though it was a gorgeous day and she loved the feel of the sun on her skin and wind in her hair, she decided to put the top up.

In case of sudden showers.

Or in case a certain delicious-looking blue-eyed bachelor strolled into the parking lot.

Just her luck. The top got stuck halfway up.

"Need any help?"

Even worse. Suddenly Andrew Clark was standing in the sunshine beside her car offering to come to her rescue. All six glorious, gorgeous, garden-loving feet of him.

Why else would he be at Patches fondling the rosemary? Unless he was a garden imposter. Suddenly, she had to find out.

"Do you cook with herbs?"

To her enormous surprise, Andrew Clark threw back his head and roared with laughter.

"As a matter of fact, I do."

"So do I." She was surprised and pleased, though why his cooking habits pleased her, she didn't have a clue. "I adore lemon basil chicken."

"Chicken's good with rosemary, too."

"So are nuts."

"Nuts?"

"Pecans and walnuts. You know. With butter and red pepper. As an appetizer. For holidays and open houses."

He cleared his throat. "Why don't you pop it up?"

"Pop it up?"

"Your trunk. To see if I can get that top up."

As Andrew's head disappeared into her trunk, Rue wondered at his sudden turnaround. The man who could hardly say "boo" to her was very much at ease talking about cooking.

But holidays stopped him cold. She wondered if his reputation for being a loner extended to Thanksgiving and Christmas. She didn't like to think of anybody sitting home alone on those holidays. Especially this man who was now whistling.

Her unexpected tenderness toward him took Rue by surprise. When he lifted his head and smiled at her, she was even more surprised. There was a streak of grease on his cheek, and Rue felt a not-so-motherly urge to wipe it off.

"I'll have you going in a jiffy," he said, after fiddling with the roof.

Thank goodness he quickly vanished into the bowels of her car. Thank goodness he didn't stare at her long enough to heighten her blush. He already had her *going.*

Oh, well, she could always blame her blush on the exertion of age.

While Rue was becoming more and more aware of him, Andrew was back at ease. And why not? After all, this was a man whose life was fast, high-performance cars, including the No. 402—Garrett's much vaunted race car.

She wondered what was really behind Andrew's cool blue eyes and endearing smile. Was he really shy with women, or was he more like Rue than she'd imagined—presenting a false front to the world while keeping his true self under wraps?

She was grateful she didn't have time to speculate. Andrew popped the lid of her trunk back down, strolled around the convertible and leaned in the window. Much too close for comfort. Furthermore, he now had that mussed look Rue loved—shirt slightly rumpled, grease on his cheek, his sandy, silver-streaked hair falling across his forehead. Rue felt hot down to the tips of her toes.

"Let's give it another try," he said. "Shall we?"

It took her a minute to realize he was talking about the convertible's top. Right before she disintegrated under his laser-like gaze, she pressed a button and the top of her convertible slid into place.

"Yippee! It works. Boy, you're good with your hands."

To her consternation, Andrew Clark took a step back as if he'd stepped into an ant hill. When would she ever learn to think before speaking?

"I was talking about with cars, of course." Andrew still looked as if he'd rather have his teeth drilled than talk to her. Instead of letting it go, Rue took that as a challenge. "Didn't I see in the paper recently that you're restoring a vintage racing car?"

Andrew visibly relaxed. "The Zakara garage restored it. When it went up for sale, I jumped at the chance to buy it. The Novi is just a hobby." That smile again. "You're welcome to stop by the garage and see it."

He was both enigmatic and charming. Was he flirting with her? Issuing an invitation? Rue felt herself getting flushed. Of course, she had to be mistaken. If reserved Andrew Clark was flirting with in-your-face Rue Larrabee, it had to be an accident.

"I might just take you up on that sometime." She flashed him a return smile. "Thanks for getting my top up. I'm lucky you happened to be here."

"I sometimes come here on my lunch break. You might even say I ran away." His boyish grin made her pulse race. Good lord. A man who could charm with such subtlety was bound to be lethal.

"Sometimes I'd like to run away, too. What are you running from, Andrew?"

"I'd rather take a beating than stand in a lineup of bachelors at Patsy's event tonight. Gardening unclutters my mind."

"Mine, too. Good luck tonight. Maybe you'll end up with a real winner."

"That's not my kind of luck with the opposite sex."

Rue was actually enjoying her conversation with Andrew. She would have said more, but his cell phone rang. With a wave, she pulled out of her parking space at Patches. Though he was already deep in conversation when she drove off, she could feel him watching her. It was like being under the beams of stage lights.

Oh, this man was dangerous. He challenged every one of Rue's notions about herself. The woman who wouldn't touch a man with a ten-foot pole because she always got burned was suddenly thinking about putting her hand back in the fire.

She had to put Andrew Clark out of her mind. Immediately.

BY THREE-THIRTY, Rue realized *immediately* was not quite the time frame she'd need for pushing Andrew Clark off her radar. She'd done nothing except think of him ever since she'd left Patches. Planting daffodils had done nothing to take her mind off the man. Granted, it was early for bulb planting, but she'd had to do something to stay busy. Besides, she hardly ever followed rules, gardening or otherwise.

She wondered if *over forty* was some kind of diabolical trap that made women go crazy. Then she wondered what kind of silly woman sat on a garden stool in front of her daffodil beds thinking such thoughts instead of doing the right thing—thanking Andrew for fixing the top on her convertible.

She'd take him some cookies. After all, he'd said to come by and see the Novi. And if he wasn't at FastMax, she'd leave them and come home, conscience clear. She still had plenty of time before Mellie arrived with Lily. Rue hurried inside to shower and change before she got cold feet.

ANDREW'S TRIP TO Patches might have done the usual relaxation trick if he hadn't run in to that strangely disturbing redhead. Back in the pre-race hubbub at FastMax, he realized he was hungry. If his mind hadn't been occupied by Rue, he'd have remembered to pick up a late-lunch hamburger on his way home from the garden center.

He rummaged in his desk drawer and came up with a pack of peanut butter crackers, which he hastily ate before returning the call to sponsor Mel Springer, CEO of Country Bread. An hour and three phone calls later, he was prowling the floor like a jungle cat when his stepson clapped him on the shoulder. "Get your butt out of here and unwind before we all get the jitters."

"Too much to do."

"Take the Novi for a spin. We've got everything covered."

Taking the antique race car for a drive might just be the answer. If ever a man needed relaxation, it was Andrew. He handled—and welcomed—the challenges and tensions of preparing for a NASCAR race, but tonight he'd be sweating under bright lights while women bid on him. A horrifying thought, even if it was for charity. Maybe nobody would bid and he'd be off the hook. He'd just write a big check, then leave.

He was running his hands over the sleek fender of the Novi when he heard the female voice.

"Yoo-hoo! Is anybody here?"

It was the Larrabee woman, surely here to drive him crazy. No sooner had he recognized the voice than she pranced into his shop, all bright colors and big attitude, red hair, oversized yellow T-shirt, black pants with yellow and pink flowers plus some kind of Zen symbol running up one leg and high-topped pink sequined tennis shoes that looked like they belonged on a performer in a punk rock band. Good lord!

Even worse, earplugs were removed, tire irons clanked to the floor, hydraulics shut off and the TV volume went from full blast to mute in less time than it took to say "a woman's in the garage." Everybody from crew chief to mechanic momentarily ceased activity to gawk, an unprecedented event.

"Hi!" Rue's big smile included every man in the garage. Half of them all but swooned. "The door was open so I just barged right in."

Before he could say anything, Rue waggled a foil-wrapped package at him.

"I brought cookies. Homemade chocolate chip. To say thank you for fixing my top."

Then, lord help him, if she didn't blush. Fascinated, he watched the color diffuse her cheeks. The blush made her look lovely and innocent, appealing in ways that could knock a man right off his feet. Andrew drew himself back from that train of thought.

"Those cookies smell good."

Smiling, she whipped off the foil and handed him one. "Fresh from the oven."

What was he supposed to do? Say something nice about a woman who cooks. If he believed the men at the track, few of them did anymore. Grace was the exception rather than the rule.

Painfully aware that he had an avid audience, all of them probably storing up smart remarks for later, Andrew took a bite and thought the cookies were delicious. But he didn't say so. And now he felt guilty. What was it about the opposite sex that always made him feel guilty or sorry or clumsy? Maybe he'd drive by the bookstore and get one of those books that would tell him what to say when the last woman on earth he'd pick if he was in his right mind had marched into his garage and brought all activity to a standstill.

Everybody in the shop was watching to see what he'd do next. He glared at his men. "Don't you have something to do?"

Suddenly everybody got busy and the decibel level rose

from zero to almost earsplitting in three seconds flat. Still Rue was watching him with such bright expectation that suddenly he did the only thing a gentleman could do.

"I was going for a drive. Would you like to come?"

"Me? You're asking me to ride with you?"

"Yes." He couldn't back out now. Saying no to her would be like telling a kid there was no Christmas.

"Oh, wow! Wait till I tell the girls at the shop."

Now look what he had done. His ineptness with women had driven him to something that would make him the topic of beauty-shop gossip. Not to mention the teasing from his own garage.

Still, the only gentlemanly thing was to set his cookies on a shelf and forget about driving the Novi. When he opened the door for her, his men let out a cheer. He might have to kill every last one of them.

"We're going in a pickup truck," he told Rue. "And besides, I'm not a driver anymore."

"I know. But you used to be."

Had she followed his career? Clipped pictures from the paper? Seen that he was but a shadow to the blazing stars of Dean and Patsy? He was too shy to ask. Still, it felt good to know that she remembered.

Thankfully, Rue was not the kind of woman who chattered every breath. She faced forward, occasionally smiling and waving to somebody she saw on the street, a nice, friendly thing to do. Besides, he was beginning to feel comfortable around her. A man could probably get used to the pink sequined tennis shoes. That is, if he wanted to.

"Is there anywhere in particular you'd like to go?"

"It's your drive, Andrew. I'm just tagging along."

"You don't seem much like a tag-along kind of woman."

"Underneath all this flashy garb is a quiet woman."

"Hearth and home?"

"Yeah. You might say I'm a stay-at-home kind of gal."

Was there a bit of longing in her voice, a hint of unfulfilled dreams? And why was he wondering? Idle curiosity, he told himself. Nothing more.

Though, what was that perfume she was wearing? It made him think of sitting on a front porch swing in the moonlight, soft music coming through the porch speakers, a soft woman in his arms.

"When you were young, did you ever imagine you'd be where you are today?" he asked.

She flashed him a smile. "You're a deep kind of guy, aren't you?"

"I like to think things through."

"I grew up here and always wanted to live here, but not necessarily alone. What about you, Andrew? Did you imagine yourself as owner of FastMax with a driver who would win the Sprint Cup championship?"

"A man with racing in his blood always dreams of the championship."

He'd dreamed of other things, too—a home with a good woman at his side, but he kept that information inside. Already, he'd revealed more of himself than he thought he should. Rue seemed to have cast some sort of spell over him.

Fortunately, she'd stopped digging into his dreams and had spotted Joe's Ice Cream Parlor.

"Oh, look. I love soft serve ice cream. Do you mind if we stop?"

"Not at all." In fact, he was relieved to be out of the close cab where Rue's appeal was bordering on downright danger-ous. He parked beside the small ice cream shack, and they sat at a wooden picnic table under the awning eating two cones of soft serve, their only conversation an occasional comment about the taste and texture of ice cream, the rightness of a cool snack in the summer.

He was holding the door for her to climb back into the truck when suddenly she put her hand on his cheek.

"You have ice cream. There."

Both her voice and touch were whisper-soft. She was close, the smell of her perfume sweet in the summer air. Awareness jolted Andrew. For a small eternity, he was trapped in the softness of her touch, unable to speak or move. When he finally made what he hoped to be a discreet move backward, Rue was left with her hand still raised, touching nothing but hot air.

The moment deserved to be written up as Most Awkward Move a Man Ever Made with a Woman. Andrew could have kicked himself.

Instead, he wiped the ice cream off his cheek and said, "I guess we should get back."

"Yes. We should."

The drive back to FastMax wasn't nearly as comfortable as the drive to Joe's. In fact, he'd rather have been anywhere than in the cab of his pickup with a woman who had suddenly lost all interest in speaking to him.

"Thanks for the ride, Andrew."

"You bet."

He was so glad for it all to be over, he'd lost his appetite for chocolate chip cookies. Thank goodness his men had eaten them anyway. No more reminders of Rue.

Except one. His lack of ease around her.

That evening, after he'd dressed in his tuxedo for the dratted bachelor auction, an hour too early as usual, he drove to the bookstore and bought *How to Talk to Women* by Dr. Sylvia Feldman. He sank into an overstuffed chair in a quiet reading corner of the store and opened the book.

"Inside every man is the hero he wants to be," Dr. Sylvia advised. *Yeah, right.*

"Overcome your greatest fear by facing it head-on," the good doctor blithely told her readers.

"We all know how that turned out, don't we, Dr. Sylvia."

Good lord. In addition to getting trussed in a penguin suit to be sold like a slab of meat, he was talking to himself. Andrew hurried from the bookstore, threw the book onto his truck's seat and drove off to face the music.

CHAPTER FOUR

IF RUE HADN'T BEEN such a fan and friend, she would never have turned the local TV station to coverage of NASCAR's Date With a Bachelor Auction. Every encounter she had with Andrew Clark turned into a total embarrassment. She wanted no more reminders.

But here she was in a clean pair of sweats with her feet propped up, a cool glass of lemonade on the table beside her recliner, a plastic dish of cookies and a coloring book on the sofa beside Lily, while NASCAR bachelors lined up to be auctioned off to the highest bidder.

They had to use the term *bachelor* lightly, because Patsy's husband, Dean Grosso, was front and center. Amidst howls of laughter and wild cheers, Patsy paid a princely sum for her husband.

Next up was Bart Branch, who took to the stage as naturally as if he were born there. Lily was beginning to nod over her coloring book, so Rue carried the child into her bedroom and tucked her in.

"Sweet dreams, princess."

Leaving the night-light on, Rue stood in the doorway long enough to make sure Lily had settled in, then she tiptoed back to the den, sank into her chair and watched a parade of NASCAR drivers good-naturedly pitching in for charity.

Finally, the man who had given Rue indigestion all evening came on stage. At least, that's what she was calling the funny feeling in the pit of her stomach. Andrew looked like he'd rather be anywhere except on center stage being bid off to a gaggle of screaming women. The sight of him took Rue's breath.

She stood up. Her glass was nearly empty. She'd go to the kitchen and pour herself some more lemonade. She'd cut a lemon into slices so she could put one on the rim of the glass. She'd take extra time washing the lemon juice off her hands. She'd do anything except sit in front of her TV drooling over a man she didn't dare want, a man who couldn't even stand for her to wipe ice cream off his face.

Instead, Rue found her feet glued to the floor. The bachelors were wearing tuxedos. It wasn't fair that Andrew Clark looked just as good in formal dress as he did in jeans with grease on the pocket.

Maybe even better. He looked worth at least a million dollars. The bidding for Andrew was hot and heavy. Of all people, Sheila Trueblood kept coming back to top every bid.

What in the world was going on? Didn't she have enough running Maudie's Diner? And wasn't she turning down Gil Sizemore's invitations right and left? What did she want with that long, tall, blue-eyed drink of water named Andrew Clark?

Not that Rue was thirsty. At least not for that particular kind of drink. In her experience, men that handsome can love only one person—themselves. Though Andrew didn't seem the least bit conceited, Rue had been wrong before.

Boy, had she been wrong!

"Sold!" The auctioneer brought the gavel down. "To Sheila Trueblood."

Sheila, dressed in a green sequined blouse that set off her flaming red hair, hurried onstage to claim her prize. When she threw her arms around him, Andrew drew back like a man electrocuted.

Rue couldn't have left the room if firemen were storming her doors to drag her from a burning house.

The TV panned in for a close-up as Sheila leaned toward Andrew. Was she going to kiss him? Or was she only planning to whisper in his ear?

Either way, Rue didn't want to know. At least, that's what she told herself as she stormed from her den and into the oasis of her kitchen. Calm green tiles. A neat row of hanging pots and pans with copper bottoms. Fresh roses on the table.

Grabbing lemons from the refrigerator, Rue set about making a fresh pitcher of lemonade. But no matter how much she sliced and diced, she couldn't get the image out of her mind—Sheila whispering sweet nothings in Andrew's ear.

"Sweet nothings, my foot." Disgusted with herself, she stomped to the sugar bowl and dumped sugar into her lemonade. The sweeter the better. Anything to keep her from turning into a bitter old woman.

Mercifully, the doorbell rang, saving Rue from uncomfortable introspection. It was Mellie coming to get Lily.

"I just made a pitcher of lemonade. Won't you have some?"

Mellie perched on the edge of her chair like an exotic bird that might take flight any minute while Rue poured two glasses of lemonade.

"I hope Lily didn't give you any trouble. Everybody's been so kind to me, I don't want to take advantage."

"Lily is an angel. Listen, sweetie, being a single working mother can be hard. Call me anytime you need a babysitter or a shoulder to cry on."

"Thanks, Rue. I'm settling in just fine." Mellie ran her hands through her spiky hair. "I should get Lily."

Lily looked so endearing, a sleepy-eyed bundle against Mellie's shoulder, Rue wondered what she'd been missing all those years. Motherhood. Chocolate-smeared hugs and sticky kisses. Footed pajamas and bedtime stories. Lullabies and rocking chairs.

It was too late for all that. Still, it would be nice to have someone to come home to, someone to share the laughter as well as the tears. As she said goodbye to Lily and Mellie, Rue wondered if there was such a thing as a second chance for her.

RESPONDING TO A phone call from Sheila for an emergency meeting of the Tarts at the diner, Rue found herself at Maudie's the next evening. When she arrived, every one of them had a grin as big as Texas. Something was up.

When Sheila saw her, she yelled, "Rue, about time!"

It didn't take a Philadelphia lawyer to figure out why Sheila looked so excited. She'd won Andrew Clark at the bachelor's auction. Obviously, she wanted to share the good news.

For once, Rue was not eager to cheer Sheila on. Not that she begrudged her. For goodness sake, Sheila deserved a date with a handsome man. Even if he was at least twice as old as Sheila.

But why couldn't it have been some *other* handsome man?

"Have a seat, Rue." Sheila popped up like she owned the restaurant. Which, of course, she did. "We have good news."

"I know. I saw the auction on TV last night." Rue gave Sheila her best smile, then reached for the plate of fried chicken.

"Isn't it wonderful!" This from Daisy, who looked as pleased as if Andrew Clark had personally agreed to go to Lamaze classes with her and be a stand-in father for her baby.

"It's great," Rue said. "Congratulations, Sheila."

The rest of the women began to laugh. Rue didn't see anything all that hilarious. "Am I missing something?"

"Yeah, but not for long," Sheila said, and there was another round of chuckles. "Rue, I didn't bid on Andrew for me. I was front woman for the Tuesday Tarts. We won him for *you*."

Rue was so flustered she didn't know whether she was relieved or mad.

"You've wasted your money. I'd as soon be strapped to a hair dryer and be thrown in a hot tub as go on a date."

Grace put on a pretty pout. "You're a nice woman and my father-in-law's a nice man. I postponed making a batch of petit fours for the Fornightly Musicale to come over here and ask you to give him a chance, Rue. What's the harm in one date?"

"You know I never go out, Grace. I don't know the first thing about dating. I'd make a complete fool of myself. Besides, doesn't your father-in-law think he's been bid off to another, *much younger* redhead?"

"Oh, don't worry about that. Patsy will handle it," Sheila said.

"It's like this, Rue. It took an act of God to get Andrew to agree to being auctioned off. If you back out, you're going to hurt his feelings."

"Hurt his feelings? Seems to me, he'd be relieved."

"My reserved brother has braved the public spotlight for my favorite charity. If you back out on the date, word will get out all over town. He'll be humiliated and hurt."

Rue had rather coat herself with honey and walk into a den of bears than hurt anybody's feelings. Besides, her friends had thought they were doing her a real favor. And she knew for a fact that with a race this weekend, Patsy wouldn't even be here if she didn't consider this fix-up date between her brother and Rue to be important.

Rue didn't want to disappoint any of them. "All right, then.

I'll take his call and we'll see what happens." The women let out a whoop of triumph. "Listen, this is just one date. That's all."

"Yeah," Sheila said, "but what a guy."

"A real hunk," Daisy added.

"A prince." Grace was positively gleeful.

"Good grief, the next thing I know all of you will be picking out bridesmaids dresses."

"I saw some on sale at the bridal shop," Patsy said, and Rue threw a roll at her.

Everyone settled in to give Rue dating advice, but her mind was on other things. Obviously, Andrew Clark didn't need to auction himself off to get a woman, even if he was as awkward as a four-legged chicken around the opposite sex.

Rue was a charity date. That was all.

She could handle that.

CHAPTER FIVE

ANDREW HAD SPENT AN incredibly hectic day seeing to last-minute details. His team was already in Indianapolis, and he'd be flying out early tomorrow in his private jet.

He got a pepperoni-and-sausage pizza from the freezer and stuck it in the oven. While it was heating, he unwound from an intense and very long day of race-related business by thinking of the perfect sunny spot in his garden for the rosemary he'd bought at Patches. By the end of December, the perennial herb would be big enough to string with small Christmas lights.

When his doorbell rang, he wondered who would be coming by so late. It was his sister in heels and a pale gray suit that probably cost more than his flat-screen TV.

What was going on? She usually called before a visit.

"You look great, Patsy." He kissed her cheek. "What's up? Would you like some tea?"

"Yes, please."

She followed Andrew to the kitchen and watched while he got down the tea he kept especially for her and then made it exactly as she liked, no sugar, lots of milk.

"Is everything all right? Is Dean okay?"

"Everything's fine. We're great." Patsy sipped her tea with maddening slowness. "This is not about me. It's about you."

"I was afraid of that."

"Don't look so crestfallen, Andrew. The world hasn't come

to an end. I just popped by to let you know you won't be taking Sheila Trueblood on a date."

"Great. I'm glad she backed out. If she wants her money back, I'll be glad to donate whatever she paid to the NASCAR charities fund."

"She didn't back out. She was bidding for the Tuesday Tarts." Andrew groaned. That couldn't be good. When women formed groups, they were up to something. "You'll be taking out another wonderful redhead with a heart of gold."

"If you have to sell her that hard, she must have a few teeth missing."

"She has all her teeth. In fact, she's gorgeous."

"Patsy, if this is a guessing game, I'm not in the mood." Andrew checked his pizza. It was bubbling, so he grabbed an oven mitt and took it out.

"The woman you'll be taking out is Rue Larrabee."

Andrew almost dropped his pizza. Why had he never noticed how much that name made Rue sound like a saloon girl in one of the John Wayne Westerns he loved to watch? By himself. Nothing but a beer and a good dog to keep him company. If he had a dog.

What more could a man need?

"You're going to like her, Andrew. She's like you. Straightforward. No games and lies. You both needed a push in the right direction."

It was funny how you could live in a small town and hardly ever run in to somebody you knew, then all of sudden that person was popping in and out of your life with the regularity of the stubborn mole who kept tunneling through your yard snatching your hosta lilies and making your life a gardener's nightmare. Obviously, God had a sense of humor.

"Don't you even think about saying *no,* Andrew. Rue is already expecting your call. If you don't call, you'll hurt her feelings."

Andrew was not the kind of man to run roughshod over anybody's feelings. In jeans, boots and a jacket filled with NASCAR patches, he might look like a tough guy with nothing but race cars on his mind. In fact, just the opposite was true. In coveted and rare moments when he was home long enough to enjoy his gardens and solitary evenings, he did some heavy thinking.

His introspection had led Andrew to believe there was no such thing as coincidence. Were recent signs pointing him toward something new?

"Andrew? Say something."

"Don't worry, Patsy. I'll uphold my end of the bargain."

Patsy's visit left Andrew unable to enjoy his pizza and his late-night TV movie, *McLintock!*, starring John Wayne. Andrew's all-time favorite Western.

Furthermore, every time Maureen O'Hara came on the screen, Andrew found himself thinking about how he'd approach his date with that other redhead—Rue Larrabee.

Maybe he'd call her tomorrow from the road. He'd call her house when he figured she'd be at her beauty shop, that way he could just leave a message and hope she'd never call back.

But that would be cowardly. And not in keeping with the bargain he'd made with Patsy. Furthermore, he could hear Dr. Sylvia screaming from the pages of that dratted book on his bedside table. "Face your greatest fear."

Commitment with the wrong woman. His first wife being the prime example. That was his fear. If Dr. Sylvia was right, he needed to get off his duff and look his fear right in the eye.

He was just getting back into the groove with John Wayne when his cell phone rang. It was his crew chief.

Andrew felt reprieved. The race at Indianapolis stretched

ahead of him, not as a long, grueling weekend, but as the kind of adrenaline-high challenge he loved.

NORMALLY RUE LOOKED forward to weekends of watching the NASCAR races on TV, sometimes alone, sometimes with friends. With the charity date looming large, she almost didn't tune in. The sight of all that NASCAR activity at Indianapolis would only remind her of her jumbled-up feelings for Andrew Clark. Around him, she was as hormonal as a teenager, blushing and gushing one minute then feeling as if she had two left feet the next.

She grabbed the rest of her King Alfred daffodils and headed to her garden. By the time she got her to flowerbeds, she'd changed her mind.

Good grief. No way was she going to let a little thing like a charity date with Andrew Clark deprive her of the races. Relieved, she went inside, made a big bowl of popcorn and settled in for a marathon of breakneck speed chills and thrills, and cheering for all her favorites.

ON MONDAY MORNING after he got back from Indianapolis, Andrew ate breakfast at home so he wouldn't run in to Rue at Maudie's and blow his whole plan. Rue rattled him in ways no woman had since he was a much younger man. Just the sight of her made him feel like a teenager. He was afraid that if he saw her prancing around like the queen of Maudie's, if not the whole doggoned town, he'd blurt out that he had to date her for the sake of the children's charities—not to mention the Tuesday Tarts.

No, it was best to wait until after he'd centered himself by working through the pile of work in his office. For Pete's sake, the Pocono race was this weekend. He needed to get this Rue business over with.

He'd catch her in her shop in the late afternoon, *facing his greatest fear.* Hopefully, she'd be tired and a bit frazzled from her long day, and he might have the advantage.

Whistling, Andrew drove to FastMax. The garage was a blur of sound and motion. During racing season, there was no letup. With a race almost every weekend, the FastMax team constantly worked like a well-oiled machine.

As he entered his garage, Andrew felt a burst of pride. The gamble he'd taken last year had paid off. His challenge now was to keep Garrett in Victory Lane.

Andrew worked straight through lunch in order to catch up with telephone conferences and paperwork so he could take a break midafternoon. When the clock hands pointed to three, he tidied up and drove off to Cut 'N' Chat.

There was a parking space right across the street. He could see Rue through the shop's window, looking anything but frazzled. As a matter of fact, even at this distance she looked a bit delicious, like a generous serving of peach ice cream you'd like to savor on a hot August day.

Shaking himself loose from that ridiculous fantasy, Andrew unfolded his long legs, stepped out of his pickup and entered Cut 'N' Chat.

Every eye turned his way and all sound ceased. He felt like a prize rooster in a henhouse.

"Good afternoon, ladies." Andrew hoped he didn't look as uncomfortable as he felt.

A few women he didn't know mumbled something under their breaths that might have passed for hello, and then the decibel level in the shop rose to one similar to the speedway.

The close-up view of the good-looking, self-confident woman very much in charge of her own domain made him think of how he operated as owner of FastMax. Like him, Rue took her business seriously. His admiration for her went up two notches. Furthermore, seeing Rue reminded him of watching Maureen O'Hara do her spitfire turn in last night's John Wayne Western. Not a good sign. He wanted to find Dr. Sylvia and strangle her. Not to mention the Tuesday Tarts.

"Andrew." Rue nodded curtly. "Sit down and make yourself comfortable. I'll be with you in a minute."

She had to know why he was there, but Rue Larrabee looked none too happy to see him. In fact, she looked like she'd love to run him through with her hair-cutting scissors.

Andrew perched on a chair that felt like it had been designed for one of those silly grown-up-looking dolls with the blond ponytail and the pink plastic convertible. Rue ignored him.

With women traipsing in and out of the shop, he picked up a magazine and flipped through the pages. It was a full two minutes before he realized it contained nothing except cake recipes and articles with a variation on the theme "ten ways women can make their husbands happy." Did women believe that stuff? No wonder Andrew had such a hard time talking to them.

What was taking Rue so long? Obviously, she didn't want to talk to him any more than he wanted to talk to her. He set the magazine aside and studied the shop to see if he could learn anything about the woman. The shop was clean and well-organized. A point in her favor. It also had a down-home feeling, like Maudie's Diner. Another plus.

Andrew wished Rue would hurry up with that haircut. If he sat there much longer, he might get to thinking he knew enough about this woman to actually enjoy being with her.

Suddenly she was standing in front of him, hands on her hips. "Well? Say what you came to say and get it over with."

Not a good start. Andrew tamped down the urge to clear his throat. Would it be too much effort for Rue to take him into her office for a little privacy? Since she'd made it clear that wouldn't be happening, Andrew had no choice but to ask her out in front of witnesses. Though some might argue that the remaining customers—two geriatrics under old-fashioned hooded hair dryers and the teenager talking her head off while she was being shampooed—weren't much in the way of witnesses.

"Rue, I'd be honored if you'd have dinner with me tomorrow night. I'll pick you up at seven and we'll drive to Charlotte."

"Is this a bachelor's auction date?"

"Yes."

"I don't have time for dating. Let's call that drive to get soft serve ice cream our *date,* and we'll be through with the whole charade."

Any other man would tell himself he'd fulfilled his obligations and walk out. But this woman was challenging him, and Andrew never backed down from a challenge.

"I can't do that."

"Can't or won't?"

"Won't."

"You're stubborn as a mule."

"Looks like that makes us two of a kind."

To his surprise, Rue laughed. "All right, then. Pick up a couple of hamburgers, bring them back here tomorrow night around six and we'll get this so-called date over with."

"Done."

Andrew would have offered a handshake to seal the deal, but he didn't want a replay of what happened at Joe's. Being up close to Rue was dangerous. She smelled nice, sweet and spicy, like his Gertrude Jekyll rose. Her skin looked soft, too, and very inviting.

Andrew hurried from the shop feeling cheated. It was the same uncomfortable position he'd often found himself in during his fifty-one years.

He vowed he was going to do something about it. He didn't know what, just yet, but he'd think of a plan.

No sooner was Andrew out of the shop than the phone rang. Rue picked up and noted the caller was Maudie's Diner.

"Did Andrew ask you out?" It was Sheila, sounding breathless.

"News travels fast."

"I saw him go inside. When's the date?"

Rue gave her the details, and there was a long silence. "Sheila? Are you there?"

"You bet, I'm here. Have fun, Rue. I'm going to call Patsy."

"Sheila, wait…" Rue said, but the phone was already dead.

The shop bell tinkled as the teenager left, and the two dryers simultaneously whirred to a stop. Rue escorted Mrs. Loretta Gibbens, who couldn't hear it thunder, to her chair, while Mrs. Charlsie Wooton, whose hearing was equally bad, toddled to Daisy's chair.

"What'd Sheila say?" Daisy took out rollers and picked up her styling brush as she talked.

"That she was calling Patsy—and probably everyone else she knows." Rue wielded her brush through Mrs. Gibbens's hair as if it were an extension of her hand.

"Good. You need some help with this date."

"It's not a real date."

"I thought he was sweet."

"He was in here less than ten minutes. How could you possibly know the first thing about him?"

"I could tell."

Sweet Daisy. Always full of hope. Something they both shared.

"One of these days, a real prince is going to come along and sweep you off your feet, Daisy."

With her blond curls bobbing and dogged determination

shining in her dark eyes, Daisy took Mrs. Charlsie Wooton's tip and stuffed it into the drawer of her styling table.

"One will come for each of us, Rue."

Rue gave Daisy a hug. "Lock up after me, sweetie." Then she took Mrs. Loretta's Gibbens's arm and helped her to her ancient sedan.

"Be careful, hon." Rue yelled loud enough for the old woman to hear. "See you next Monday." Then she stood there waving until Mrs. Gibbens safely maneuvered her car away from the curb and crept off down the street.

ANDREW HAD BEEN sitting in his truck across the street from Cut 'N' Chat for ten minutes, listening to the radio turned low to a country/Western station and playing along on his harmonica.

He'd needed time to think before he reentered the controlled chaos of his garage, and this seemed as good a place as any. When Rue came out of the shop, he switched his radio off—and heard every word she said to the old lady.

At the precise moment Rue stood on the street, waving at the departing sedan, Andrew knew he was in trouble. Rue was the kind of woman he could fall for, one with a generous spirit and a kind heart.

The date loomed before him as a sort of Waterloo. When Andrew drove off, he told himself that if he didn't want to get burned again, he'd have to handle Rue with caution.

CHAPTER SIX

ON TUESDAY MORNING, Rue dressed in her bright blue blouse, ankle pants, espadrilles and earrings the size of Montana. She had no intention of doing anything different simply because she had a charity date with Andrew Clark that evening. And she certainly had no intention of repeating her mistake in front of Joe's. As far as she was concerned, Andrew would be the untouchable.

She picked up doughnuts and was relieved not to see him in Maudie's. Daisy didn't comment when Rue walked into the shop, set down the box of doughnuts and donned her styling apron.

As hard as Rue tried to make this Tuesday just another ordinary day, she found herself getting flushed thinking about the way Andrew had smiled at her from under the hood of her Mustang. And she dropped her brush when she remembered the way he'd looked with ice cream on his cheek or sitting on her beauty shop chair—uncomfortable, staunch and endearing.

It was the *endearing* part that got to her. If she weren't careful, she might start expecting more than hamburgers from Andrew Clark. She might expect him to hold her hand and tell her she was pretty. She might expect a smile that felt intimate. She might even expect a kiss. Not a perfunctory kiss on the cheek but a real one. The kind she sometimes still dreamed about when she was sitting up late watching *Pretty Woman* or *An Affair to Remember*.

At five the shop door burst open and in trooped Patsy, Grace and Sheila, their arms laden with bags and boxes.

"Surprise," yelled Sheila.

"Are you here to watch me make a fool of myself tonight?"

"We're here for your makeover." Sheila jerked a pair of gold sling-back stiletto heels out of a box. "We'll start with these."

"Good grief, I'm not wearing those. I'd fall and break my fool neck."

Ignoring her, Sheila said, "Daisy, grab your brush. We've got to do something with Rue's hair."

"What's wrong with my hair?" Rue glimpsed herself in the mirror. The heat of exertion had caused her curls to spring every which way. Her hair looked like a Brillo pad.

"You won't be needing this old ammonia-smelling thing." Daisy removed Rue's apron, then led her to her styling station. "Sit down. I'm going to froufrou you."

"I don't want to be froufroued. This is not a real date."

"After Andrew gets a gander at you in my dress, it'll be real." Patsy opened her bag and pulled out a green, slinky dress with most of the front and the back missing.

"Good grief, Patsy. Why aren't you home getting ready for the race at Pocono?"

"Dean can handle things for a while. Besides, all work and no play makes Patsy a dull girl, and we all know that's not true." The rest of the women whooped. "Here. Put this on."

"I'm not wearing that. I'd look like somebody who hasn't had sex in fifteen years and can't wait to jump Andrew's bones."

Patsy grinned.

"Exactly," Grace said.

"Oh, hush up," Rue told her. But she had to admit that Daisy had done wonders with her hair.

And the dress didn't look half-bad, either. Especially with the shoes. Plus the dangling rhinestone earrings Grace added. In fact, Rue hadn't felt this feminine in a long time.

"You look fabulous," Patsy told her and everyone cheered.

"But don't you think it's way over-the-top for hamburgers?" Nobody said anything, which started to arouse Rue's suspicions. "What if I ruin the dress? It probably cost an arm and a leg."

Patsy kissed her on the cheek. "Dresses can be replaced. Friends can't."

"Lord, look at the clock," Sheila said. "Let's get out of here. It's almost showtime."

It was ten minutes till six. Rue wondered if Andrew would be prompt. She also wondered if she had time to change back into her blouse and pants.

But what if Andrew arrived with the hamburgers while she was stripping?

"Good grief."

Rue perched on the edge of a chair feeling like an imposter. When the bell over her shop's door tinkled, she nearly jumped out of the skimpy dress. *Oh, help.*

Ruining Patsy's dress was the least of her worries. In his tuxedo, Andrew looked like something good to eat.

No wonder her friends wanted to froufrou her. They *knew.* Wait till Rue finished with them.

"Hello, Rue. You look very pretty tonight."

Only three minutes into her date, and already one wish had been granted. Furthermore, there was no artifice in Andrew. His smile was sweet, shy and sincere.

"Thank you. It's the dress. It belongs to your sister."

"It looks like it was made for you."

Genuinely touched, Rue covered her feelings by redirecting the conversation. "I told Patsy the dress was too fancy for hamburgers. Just bring the bag to my office. We'll eat at my desk."

"That won't be necessary."

"I'd hate to balance my food on my lap. And I don't want to spill mustard on your sister's dress."

"I'm sure she wouldn't mind." He examined her with the thoroughness he'd probably use in assessing a good race car. Rue felt her skin heating up. "That shade of green suits you."

They stared at each other, neither saying another word. When the shop bell tingled, Andrew took a step back and Rue caught her first full breath since he'd entered her salon.

"What in the world?" Rue chastised herself for forgetting to hang out the Closed sign.

"Our dinner," Andrew said.

Astounded, Rue watched while caterers set up a table complete with white linen cloth, roses, candlelight and champagne. She hadn't had champagne since she was doing a taste test for her unfortunate wedding reception. *Unfortunate* because it never took place.

Next came the food. Instead of hamburgers, Rue would be dining on lobster with drawn butter—her favorite food in the world—escargot and asparagus tips, endive salad and flaky, buttery rolls.

Rue wondered if the caterers would stay. It would certainly make this so-called date easier.

When the last spotless glass was in place, the head caterer turned to her. "What time do you want us back in the morning to clean up?"

"Seven-thirty will be fine."

She could do most of it later this evening, which would make it easy for the caterers to be out of her shop before the first customer arrived. Dinner shouldn't take more than an hour. An hour and a half, at most. Rue would be home watching TV by nine o'clock.

From her CD player, Willie Nelson crooned "Nothing I Can Do About It Now." It fit Rue so perfectly, it ought to be her theme song. Her boat had sailed a long time ago. It was too late to try to climb on board now.

With the caterers gone, Andrew didn't seem to know what to say or do. After he had planned such an elaborate surprise, the least Rue could do for him was provide appropriate music.

She risked standing in her revealing dress and high heels. As she crossed the room, she could feel Andrew watching her. His gaze made her feel desirable for the first time in years.

A bit self-conscious, she quipped, "I'm changing my tune."

She and her customers were partial to country/Western, but it didn't go with lobster and champagne. Rue flipped through a stack of CDs and chose a romantic ballad.

Out of the corner of her eye, she saw Andrew, still watching. When she'd tried to wipe ice cream off his cheek, he'd probably thought she was using that as an excuse to touch him. She hoped her CD selection didn't give him the idea that she was expecting more than a great meal and good company. She hoped he didn't think she wanted to turn their charity date into a romantic encounter.

"That's nice music," he said. "Frank Sinatra?"

"Yes. I always did love Old Blue Eyes." She looked up into Andrew's laser-blue eyes and felt herself blush. "I mean him. Frank."

He didn't have a response, and for an awkward moment Rue wondered how they would ever get through this evening together. She tore herself away from his gaze and moved toward the table.

"This looks delicious. Shall we eat before it gets cold?"

Rue had her hand on her chair when Andrew appeared and pulled it out for her. She nearly cracked up. "Thanks."

"It doesn't take much to amuse you."

"It's not you. It's Sheila. She said she'd kill me if I pulled out my own chair."

"It looks like I've saved you."

His statement was so loaded with double meanings, Rue almost cried. But as Andrew filled their glasses with champagne, she could find no guile in him. And she was checking. Hard.

It wasn't that she needed saving. She had a good life and she was content. But every now and then she got the what-if blues. What if she could turn back the clock? What if she could somehow be transformed into the kind of woman who would attract somebody wonderful?

Two was a much cozier number than one.

That kind of thinking was dangerous. Especially since Mooresville's most appealing bachelor was sitting across the table from her.

"It looks like you did save me." Rue kept her tone light. "Thanks."

"My pleasure. I don't get much opportunity to save women."

"What about the day at Patches?"

"That was your car."

"Actually, it was me. What if you hadn't come along? What if it had started raining? I would have been drenched. I might even have caught pneumonia and died."

Andrew threw back his head and roared with laughter. "The next time I need something to feel good about, I'm calling you to see if you need me to check under your hood. Besides, you might bring me some more chocolate chip cookies."

"My hood's so old it needs regular tune-ups."

"Most old cars do. More butter?"

It seemed Andrew was bent on rescuing her from her double entendres. When he passed a small dish to her, Rue dipped her lobster inside. Butter dripped onto his hand, and Rue felt herself getting flushed.

She blamed it on the candlelight.

Holding her glass to him, she said, "I think I'll have more champagne, too."

He refilled both their glasses, then lifted his. "To NASCAR."

Rue clicked her glass with his. "To good friends."

"To the bachelors' auction."

"To...good hair."

By the fourth toast, Rue was giggling. She was actually having fun. Andrew was turning out to be good company. She kicked off her shoes.

"I think I'll have some more of that bubbly."

"Glad to oblige."

Andrew refilled their glasses then tossed his tie onto Rue's styling chair. For some reason, she found that hilarious. In fact, everything about dining on lobster and champagne in the middle of Cut 'N' Chat suddenly struck Rue as funny... and amazing.

Here she was, the most jilted woman in town, dining in candlelight with a man who had told her she was pretty, told her that she made him feel good. This was the kind of amazement she knew wouldn't let her sleep tonight. Long after her head touched the pillow, she'd be replaying every detail of the evening.

Under the influence of candlelight and champagne, music and the steady regard of Andrew Clark, Rue felt revitalized, a woman for whom a miracle could occur when she least expected it. They talked about Garrett's chances at the upcoming race in Pocono and the fact that Jeb Stallworth would be a hard driver to beat. They talked of gardening and movie classics and the beauty of North Carolina in the spring. They discussed their love of books and music and fast cars. They shared a love of the South in general and Southern cooking in particular, especially with home-grown herbs. They discovered they both thought unkindness was the worst trait a person could have. Worse even than sloth and envy.

So filled with excitement she couldn't sit still, Rue jumped up and did an impromptu waltz around the room. She felt like a woman who might just reach out and take exactly what she wanted.

At the moment, what she wanted happened to be sitting in a chair two feet from her, watching her in the way of a man who fully appreciates what he is seeing.

"Want to join me?"

"I don't dance. I think I'll just sit here and enjoy watching."

"It's better with two."

Andrew stood up and pulled her into his arms. "Isn't everything?" His voice was no more than a whisper against her hair.

Delicious shivers spiraled over Rue. She became aware of every breath, every heartbeat, every inch of skin exposed by Patsy's revealing dress.

Andrew's hands felt warm against her bare back, warm and intimate and full of promise. She loved his touch, the way his hands fit perfectly into the curve of her back, the way he pressed his cheek against hers, as if he might turn at any moment and kiss her.

On this amazing night, anything was possible.

"I thought you didn't dance," she teased.

"I don't. I'm just moving to your rhythm."

He tightened his hold and the nearness of him rocked Rue to the core. Sensations swept through her—heat, hunger and desire. Through Patsy's silky dress she was aware of every muscle in his thighs, the strength and power of his arms, the heart-thumping appeal of a chest built for comfort as well as excitement.

They waltzed around the small crowded shop where the hair dryers and styling stations and washbasins suddenly seemed magical. Andrew was a good dancer, which didn't surprise Rue. She was beginning to learn that this man did everything well.

Pressed so close they seemed to be one, Rue felt his body's rhythm, relaxed into it, reveled in it. Suddenly she was no longer the Woman Who Chose Bad Men. She was a Woman Dancing in Candlelight, a woman on the brink of knowing what it felt like to fall in love.

"I feel like Cinderella at the ball."

"Do you believe in magic, Rue?"

"I do. Call me sentimental."

"That's not what I would call you."

His footsteps slowed to a standstill and Andrew cupped her face. As he looked deeply into her eyes, she hardly dared breathe for fear the magic would vanish.

The kiss took her by surprise. Later, neither would be able to remember who started it, but both would never forget how it all ended.

At first the kiss was light, a tentative tasting as lips brushed against lips. Then he pulled her closer, deepening the kiss, and both were swept away in a firestorm of passion.

Rue's carefully built barriers tumbled. Long-held notions of being a woman spurned bit the dust. The idea that real life had passed her by reformed itself into a dream of a beautiful new boat with sails that would sweep her away to paradise.

"Rue?" Andrew didn't need to form the question. She'd known the answer even before he asked.

"Yes. Oh, yes."

There was no hesitation in the joining, no awkwardness, no

feeling of having to get to know each other. It was as if they'd been together for years, as if they'd been created especially for each other, designed specifically for this moment.

In the next hour, the Cut 'N' Chat transformed itself from Rue's work place to a place of miracles. In the rain of kisses from Andrew Clark, years of rejection and disappointment fell away. Rue felt amazement, she felt beautiful and she felt cherished.

CHAPTER SEVEN

A PERSISTENT RINGING startled Andrew awake. Sleep-fogged, he was reaching for his cell phone when his hand encountered a long curve of soft skin.

Rue's leg, draped over his hips as she slept.

His first thought was *How did that happen?* His second was a replay of vivid memories—the heated kisses, the tumultuous need, the deep desire that had reached out of nowhere and snatched them both under.

Conflicting feelings flooded Andrew. The evening had been both wonderful and terrible. Terrible because he considered himself a true gentleman, and no gentleman would take advantage of a woman who'd had too much champagne, even if she did say yes. And wonderful because he had connected with Rue on a level he hadn't thought possible. For the first time in many years, Andrew had felt appreciated for himself, exactly as he was—a no-frills, straightforward man who enjoyed the simple things of life.

Still, past experience had taught him that what you see is not always what you get. Clever women have a way of reeling you in with sweet talk before they proceed to rip you apart and try to put you back together their way.

Andrew's watch said seven. He had to get out of the beauty salon. Before long, the street would be alive with people. In fact, Al would already be cooking for his first customers at Maudie's next door.

Too, Andrew had to find out who was calling this early.

What if it was some family emergency? What if it was Garrett or the crew chief calling to report unforeseen trouble?

Taking care not to wake Rue, he gently untangled himself and then found his cell phone on the table along with their empty plates and champagne glasses. The call he'd missed was from Jim Stevens, his old pit boss who had retired to Belfast, Maine, and now spent his time rebuilding boats.

It must be urgent or Jim wouldn't be calling so early. Still, Andrew didn't want to risk waking Rue with a telephone conversation.

Briefly he thought about leaving her a note, but what would he say? *Hi, had a nice time, see you later.*

He couldn't stand there dithering. Soon the caterers would be bursting in. And he didn't have a clue how early Rue took clients. Call him old-fashioned, but he was the kind of man who worried about a woman's reputation.

He'd think about his moment of total abandon with Rue later. Now he had to find out why Jim was calling. And he had to get ready to leave for Pocono.

Holding the bell above the door so it wouldn't disturb Rue, Andrew slipped from the shop and hurried toward his car, punching Jim's number as he walked.

RUE WOKE UP IN dishabille with a horrific headache and the certainty that she had made a complete fool of herself. Furthermore, she was in the back room of her beauty shop, and she was alone. Which said it all.

Dinner with Andrew had been a present from the Tuesday Tarts. The rest…well, that had to be blamed on champagne. And long-neglected needs. There had probably been a little hope in the mix, too, but the clear light of day wiped that clean.

Men who had intentions of seeing you again didn't have sex and then disappear without a single word.

Rue tried to chalk up what had happened to an unfortunate lapse in judgment. If she didn't get off the floor, Rue was going to feel more than foolish. She was going to get caught.

Jerking on yesterday's slacks and blouse, she hurried around the shop scooping up evidence. Sheila's gold shoes by the table, one of Grace's earrings by the wash basins, Andrew's tie, for goodness sake.

Rue was standing in the middle of her shop clutching Andrew's tie and wondering where she'd dropped Grace's other earring when Sheila pranced in.

Though Sheila was holding a box, Rue could guarantee she wasn't there merely to deliver doughnuts.

"I saw your lights on." Sheila was stopped in her tracks by the sight of the meticulous Rue wearing yesterday's clothes. "Tell all."

"There's nothing to tell." Rue flushed as memories flooded her. "We had dinner. And that's all I'm saying. End of story."

"*Nothing to tell?* Is that why you're fondling Andrew's tie?"

"Oh, for Pete's sake."

Mad at herself for falling into his arms like a ripe plum, mad at Andrew for running out like a scalded dog, mad at Sheila and the Tuesday Tarts for getting her into the mess in the first place, Rue flung the tie into the top drawer of her styling table.

"I hope Andrew's tie means things got cozy," Sheila said.

Rue decided the best answer was total silence. That didn't deter Sheila one iota.

"When will you see him again?"

The way he ran off without a word, probably never. Rue wasn't about to share that information with Sheila.

"What do you mean, 'When will I see him?'" Everybody in Mooresville shows up at your diner."

"That's not what I mean, and you know it." Sheila's squinty-eyed perusal unsettled Rue. "Is that beard burn I see on your chin?"

Thank goodness the caterers arrived to clean up, and Rue was saved the further embarrassment of continuing a conversation about yet another man who hadn't bothered to tell her goodbye.

"Listen, thanks for bringing the doughnuts over."

"I'm not through with you, yet, Rue Larrabee. Don't even think about keeping secrets from us. We have our ways."

Sheila was right, of course. Since the Tarts had bought and paid for Andrew Clark, they'd think they had a vested interest in knowing every detail of his date with Rue.

She just wasn't going to think about it. In fifteen minutes, she'd be elbow-deep in permanent wave solution with Lillian Jones, the first on a full calendar of Wednesday regulars.

Rue would be like Scarlett O'Hara: she'd think about Andrew Clark tomorrow.

TRYING TO PUT HIS night at the Cut 'N' Chat out of his mind, Andrew took a quick shower, then raced to his office. His secretary brought coffee while he made phone calls.

His early morning call had been from his college room-mate, saying he was getting married. He hadn't been able to wait to share the news. The wedding would be at the beach and they were planning to honeymoon on his boat.

It was the honeymoon part that drew Andrew back into the dilemma of Rue. That's how Andrew now came to think of his ill-conceived and fatal date. Ill-conceived because he should have known better. Fatal because of what had happened after dinner.

Not only had he lost his head over a woman as unsuited to

him as a woman could be, but he'd let passion guide him instead of common sense. A man didn't have sex with a woman he had no intention of ever dating again. Obviously, he'd let the feisty redhead get under his skin.

Andrew groaned. What was he going to do now? Call and say, *I'm sorry, I didn't mean for that to happen?* She'd hate him. Call and say, *Thanks, it was great but we're completely wrong for each other.* She'd despise him. Send flowers and a note saying, *Sorry I had to rush out, but this will never work.* She'd throw rocks at his window.

As far as he could tell, there was no graceful way out. Once you became intimate, women started thinking they owned you. They started thinking of ways to change you and finagle you to the altar.

Andrew was in a lose/lose situation. He didn't want to further embarrass Rue by being uncordial, and he certainly didn't want her to get the wrong idea by being friendly. Fortunately, he'd be leaving for Pocono in less than an hour. Out of sight, out of mind.

Why didn't that plan make him feel any better?

ALL DAY WEDNESDAY, Rue half expected Andrew to call. He'd say, *I'm sorry I had to leave in such a hurry,* then he'd explain and ask when he could see her again. Or he'd call and say he had a lovely time and would she consider going to the movies with him sometime. Or he would call and simply say he'd had a great time and hoped she had, too. He'd leave the door open for future involvement when they returned from the weekend NASCAR races.

He didn't call, of course, and by the time she was putting on a nightshirt that declared Keep America Beautiful, Put a Sack over Your Head, Rue could have killed Andrew Clark.

He was just another handsome man who proved once and

for all that she was the Woman Men Loved to Dump. She didn't care if he was an important owner who had to be with his team in Pocono. The least he could have done was leave a note. And hadn't the man ever heard of cell phones?

Furious at him, even more furious at herself, she switched off the light vowing she'd never go on another date as long as she lived.

BY THURSDAY, with still no word from Andrew, Rue went from fury to gratitude that he was either already in Pocono or too busy preparing for the races to call. That afternoon she picked up Patsy's dress from the cleaners, then started to call and see if Daisy wanted to see a movie.

But another movie with a girlfriend was not what Rue wanted. Andrew had made her want things she knew she couldn't have. He'd made her take another look at the life she'd carved out for herself, and currently she didn't like what she was seeing—lonely evenings in front of the TV, Thanksgiving and Christmas and birthdays for one.

Futhermore, it was getting harder and harder to pretend that being a combination of Mother Teresa and Lucille Ball was all Rue needed.

Sighing, Rue walked home and called Patsy's cell phone, prepared to leave a message. She was surprised when Patsy answered.

"I didn't think I'd get you, Patsy."

"We're just checking in."

"I've got your dress back from the cleaners. I'll bring it by the farm when you get back from Pocono." The farm was nothing of the sort. It was merely the name Patsy used to describe the Grossos' sprawling country estate.

"So…how did it go? Was the dinner fabulous?"

"The lobster was great. You knew about it before Andrew came over."

"Of course. Grace is friends with the caterer." Patsy laughed. "The Tarts see all."

Not quite. Thank goodness.

"Listen, Patsy. About that invitation to Watkins Glen, I really can't go."

"I won't let you back out."

"I have to."

"Why?"

"Something's come up."

"Rue Larrabee, the only way I'm letting you off the hook is if you're in the hospital with fever of a hundred and ten."

"I'd be dead."

"Exactly."

"What if I just don't show up to board your plane?"

"I'll send Dean over to get you. And you know that nobody says *no* to Dean."

Rue sighed. "You're a hard woman, Patsy Clark Grosso."

"Thank you."

RUE INVITED Daisy over to watch the races on Saturday, and again on Sunday. Sitting on Rue's sofa with popcorn and lemonade on Sunday afternoon, they watched the prerace interviews. Patsy and Dean, gracious as always, answered questions about their son Kent's chances of capturing another NASCAR Sprint Cup Series championship. Recently he'd come in second at Daytona, first in Chicago and fourteenth in Indianapolis.

"We're very optimistic," Dean told the press.

But it was the interview with Andrew that had Rue glued to the set. If there was anything more enticing than a handsome blue-eyed man in a leather jacket covered with his company's logo, Rue didn't even want to think about it.

"You like him, don't you?" Daisy said.

"He's not my type."

"He's nice."

"That's just the point. What would a nice, shy man like that want with a flamboyant sexpot like me?"

"Rue, don't sell yourself short."

"How's that baby? Kicking hard?"

Daisy accepted the subject change without comment. When the "Gentlemen, start your engines" announcement was made, both women stood up and gave the rebel yell. As Kent Grosso blazed around the track, they stood up and whooped for joy. They both said they were hoping for a win for Patsy and Dean's son at Pocono. Though, truth to tell, Rue was secretly pulling for Andrew's stepson, Garrett. *No particular reason,* she told herself.

Two bowls of popcorn, two hot dogs and two slices of apple pie later, Rue escorted Daisy to her car, told her to call when she got home safely, then watched until she had backed safely out of the driveway. Though neither Kent nor Garrett had won, Rue still wore the excitement of NASCAR racing like a favorite sweater she could hug to herself long after she was in bed.

Monday evening Rue went to Patches, telling herself she needed some more bulbs and maybe one of the camellia bushes they had on sale. But the truth was, she wanted to revisit the place where she'd had her first really lovely encounter with Andrew, and maybe she was even hoping to run in to him.

Rue wanted to see for herself whether her wild imaginings of the last few days made any sense. Visions of Andrew haunted her day and night. She'd be in the midst of giving a haircut when she'd remember the feel of his hands on her skin. She'd be making a cup of tea or slicing bread when she'd get hot all over remembering how they'd been, like two people who knew each other inside and out, lovers through time reunited after centuries of being apart.

Oh, she was turning into a foolish woman. Before, she'd been able to laugh off her failures with men. She'd been able to joke with her girlfriends about her infamous escapades.

But her night with Andrew had been different. She'd let her heart get involved.

Looking back at how it had all ended, Rue didn't know whether Andrew had failed her or whether she had failed him. Maybe it was both.

Rue parked her Mustang in the Patches parking lot and hurried inside. *Forget Andrew,* she told herself. Still, she found herself remembering a certain blue-eyed bachelor in the herb section.

"Good afternoon, Miss Larrabee." It was the young horticulture student who worked at Patches in summers and holidays.

"Hey, Jonsey. What's new?"

"We got in a shipment of orchids."

"Any purple phalaenopsis?"

"We've got one purple left. You'd better hurry."

"Thanks, Jonsey."

The orchid display was stunning—white phalaenopsis and yellow oncidium, the dancing ladies. There was even a coveted cattleya. Rue targeted the orchids like a heat-seeking missile, her eyes darting among the gorgoues, exotic blooms.

"Oh, no, where's the purple phalaenopsis?"

She hadn't meant to voice her dismay aloud.

A tall man in jeans, T-shirt and baseball cap turned around, holding the purple orchid.

Andrew Clark. Heat seared Rue from the roots of her hair to the tips of her curled-up toes. She didn't know what she wanted most—to die on the spot or to wrap her arms around him and kiss him silly.

"Hello, Rue."

"I…" She put her hand on her throat to loosen the words.

One look at him and her traitorous mind replayed every erotic moment of their date. "I thought you might still be in Pocono."

"No. I got back late last night."

"Did you have a nice weekend?"

"Yes. And you?"

Just how great a weekend did he expect her to have after he'd left her without a word?

"It was great." Her smile felt so false it's a wonder her face didn't crack.

"That's nice."

For Pete's sake, if either of them said one more sentence that included *nice,* she was going to throw up on his shoes. That is, if she didn't fall to his fatal attraction first. Delicious memories assaulted her, and she felt her face going pink. Did he know he was the cause of her blush? After the way he'd left her shop, Rue didn't want to give him the satisfaction.

"I have to be going." Rue started to walk away.

"Wait." She turned back around and he held out the orchid. "Is this what you're looking for?"

Days of waiting for a call that hadn't come boiled over. "You don't have a thing I'm looking for, Andrew Clark."

Let him chew on that. Rue marched out but he caught up with her. His hand on her shoulder felt like a white-hot branding iron.

"Rue, I'm sorry about what happened."

Nothing deflates the ego faster than being told the man was sorry he had sex with you. Rue wanted to die on the spot.

"Not half as sorry as I am," she snapped.

"I didn't mean it that way."

"Forget it, Andrew. It's water under the bridge."

"Do your eyes always turn emerald when you lie?"

"Don't you dare talk to me about lying, Andrew Clark. I've

had it with men who take what they want then dump me like a sack of potatoes."

This time when she stormed off, he didn't try to follow her. Good thing, for she was so mad she wouldn't be responsible for what she did.

She was so upset she stopped at Baskin-Robbins and had a banana split. It would serve Andrew Clark right if she put on twenty pounds.

CHAPTER EIGHT

AFTER HIS SUPPER break at Patches, Andrew worked well into Monday evening. By the time Patsy arrived at FastMax, everybody had finally left the garage and he was under the hood of his Novi, trying to take his mind off his unsettling encounter with Rue at Patches. His sister had come unannounced for the second time. Was the world coming to an end?

He could guess why she was there. Since she had gone to all the trouble to lend Rue a dress, Patsy was taking some kind of unusual and nosy interest in Andrew's so-called love life.

She'd probably been the chief instigator in his dinner date with Rue in the first place.

He had no intention of talking about it. Sister or no sister. He knew she'd consider it impolite if he kept his head under the hood, but he did it anyhow.

"Hey, Patsy. What's up?"

"I have no intention of talking to the side of a car."

"This is important. Can you give me a sec?" Maybe if he kept her waiting long enough, she'd try to quit minding his business and go home.

"Get out from under that hood and face the music."

"What music?"

"You know darned good and well, Andrew Joseph Clark."

Grabbing a chamois cloth to wipe his hands, Andrew emerged from the bowels of the antique race car. One look at Patsy's face told him she was on the warpath.

"I want to know what happened on your date with Rue."

"Nothing." At least nothing that was his sister's business.

"Something must have."

Here we go again. It wouldn't be the first time a woman had aired her problems with Andrew in public.

"What did she tell you, Patsy?"

"She didn't say anything. I just know, that's all." That was a relief. Still, at Patches, Rue had barely contained her dislike of him. It wouldn't be long before the whole town caught on. "She's so upset with you that she backed out on flying to Watkins Glen with me."

Just when Andrew thought matters couldn't get worse, they had.

"I don't know why you invited her to New York." But he could certainly guess. Apparently, his sister had decided he'd been a bachelor long enough. From the looks of things, she was determined to hitch him up with somebody, come hell or high water. "Look, I know I asked to fly with you so Garrett could take my plane early, but I've changed my mind. I'll cancel my meeting and fly with Garrett and the rest of the team. Or better yet, I'll go up early with the car. That ought to fix things with Rue."

As Patsy mulled that over, she looked like a woman who had bit down on something she didn't want to chew.

"She's a wonderful woman, Andrew."

"Probably so."

"Then what's the problem?"

"There is no problem, Patsy. We had a nice dinner together. Isn't that what you wanted?"

Patsy had the good grace to squirm a bit, which had been Andrew's intent. The only way to win with his sister was to turn the tables and put her on the hot seat.

"What I want is for you to fix whatever went wrong so Rue will feel comfortable accepting my invitation. You can catch her at Maudie's tomorrow night with the Tuesday Tarts."

"If I had a clue what women want, I wouldn't be single."

"I just want you to be happy, Andrew."

"Who said I wasn't?"

"How can you be? You never go anywhere or see anybody unless it's race or family related. If you're not careful, you'll end up an old man living all by yourself."

"I've got Garrett and Grace and the kids."

"So do I. But everybody needs a partner to love."

"As much as I appreciate your concern, Patsy, it's my life, isn't it?"

His sister was nobody's fool. She changed the subject to the race at Watkins Glen.

When she left, she wasn't in a huff, but she wasn't too happy, either. Andrew could say the same for himself. Patsy had opened up a subject he'd rather forget. What to do about Rue.

Obviously, Rue was upset enough that it showed in public. Otherwise, she wouldn't have run out of Patches like her coattail was on fire.

Further proof of Rue's inability to chalk their intimacy up to a mere lapse in judgment—as Andrew was trying to do—was the fact that Patsy had marched over to FastMax and read him the riot act.

Andrew would never understand women. Why couldn't Rue figure out that he was not the kind of man to wake up a woman to give his agenda? Or take the time to leave a note when the most important thing was to save her reputation by vacating her shop before the caterers got there and half the town started arriving at Maudie's?

Heck, he wasn't even the kind of man who had sex with a woman on the first date.

Work, that was the answer. That, plus going about his business as if Rue Larrabee had never happened.

BY TUESDAY EVENING, Andrew realized the only way he could set himself free was to apologize to Rue. Though calling would be simple and much less painful than a face-to-face confrontation, Andrew liked to think of himself as a man who didn't opt for the easy way out. Besides, there was the redoubtable Dr. Sylvia, admonishing him from the pages of her self-help tome—*face your greatest fear.*

Between the Tuesday Tarts and the beauty shop grapevine, everybody in town would already know far more than they should about his date with Rue. A public personality such as Rue deserved a public apology.

And because of his sister, he knew exactly where Rue would be. Andrew walked out of his office, announced he was leaving to get dinner for everybody at Maudie's, then took orders. And a whole bunch of ribbing.

"This wouldn't have anything to do with the redhead who was in here, would it, boss?" Robbie, the brownie thief, was nobody's fool. He'd been around long enough to know about Tuesday nights at Maudie's.

The glare from Andrew shut his crew chief up.

As Andrew left FastMax he thought of the purple orchid. The purple one Rue had wanted.

He'd bought it to add to his collection, which he kept in his den near a bank of windows with plenty of eastern exposure. A true gardener with a love of seasonal bloom, he always stocked up on orchids in late summer so he'd have something blooming all winter. Nothing perked him up like coming home to the surprise of exotic blooms.

Amend that. Almost nothing. Lately—in fact, since he'd been with Rue—he'd wondered what it would be like to come home to the soft embrace of a lively, interesting, kindhearted woman. One who loved gardening and racing, classic movies and great music. And hopefully the St. Louis Cardinals.

He thought about stopping by his place to get the purple orchid as a peace offering, then decided against it. For one thing, he didn't have time. For another, a man bearing gifts would send the wrong message.

On the way to Maudie's, Andrew called to place his large take-out order. Then he started whistling. His conscience was clear as a bell.

Or, it soon would be.

TUESDAY EVENING, Rue found the Tarts holding court in the back room at Maudie's. Grace, who was catering a wedding reception, wasn't there, but Patsy, taking a supper break from working with her team, scooted over to make room for Rue. "We were just discussing our trip to New York."

"I've already told you, Patsy. I can't make it this year." Rue didn't miss the *look* that passed around the table.

"I don't know about you, Rue, but I wouldn't let any man knock me out of seeing a NASCAR race in person." Sheila grabbed some cheese and crackers from the center of the table. "I never figured you would, either."

"Who said it was a man?" Rue tried for feisty, but failed.

In addition, the door to the back room opened and in walked Andrew Clark. If ever a man was made to wear an open-necked white shirt rolled at the sleeves, he was the one. He ought to be on a billboard advertising something sensual. A men's cologne that brought women to their knees.

Every one of Rue's chimes was ringing.

"Speaking of the devil," Patsy said and waved her brother over.

"Don't." Rue grabbed her hand, but it was too late. Andrew was heading her way. She stood up to leave, but Sheila pointed to one of the empty chairs on the opposite side of the table.

Freedom lay past Sheila. Considering her starring role in the date fiasco, Sheila Trueblood wouldn't be about to aid and abet Rue in a hasty escape.

She might as well sit down and act like Andrew was any other man in Mooresville. And that was the burr under her saddle. He was anything *but*.

"Hello, ladies," Andrew said. "Rue. Patsy."

Rue nodded at him, hoping she didn't look like a woman about to jump out of her skin. But when Andrew leaned over her to kiss Patsy on the cheek, Rue had to bite her tongue to keep from groaning. The lingering fragrance of his soap washed over her, and she remembered the feel of his skin against hers, the taste, the smell, like sunshine and outdoors and desire.

"Hey, Patsy," he said.

Rue was so flustered she should hang a sign on her chest that said Woman in Flames.

She didn't know how much longer she could stand to be this close to Andrew without reaching up to touch him.

"How's it going, Andrew?" Patsy had the distinct look of a woman up to something.

"Good." Andrew straightened up but then proceeded to lean against the wall next to where Rue was sitting. The entire right side of his body was practically glued against her.

Heat seared her and she was certain her face had turned ten shades of red. If she shifted half an inch toward Patsy, she might have some breathing room, but she wasn't about to give Andrew the satisfaction of knowing what his nearness did to her.

Besides, everyone was watching.

"Listen to me," Patsy said. "Carrying on like I'm the only one in the room. You didn't come all the way over here to talk to me, did you, Andrew?"

"No."

The word was so laden with hidden meaning that Rue made the fatal mistake of looking into Andrew's eyes.

Writers might describe what happened next as drowning in a deep pool, but for Rue, the sensation was more like flying. Caught in Andrew's gaze, she imagined herself growing wings and flying far beyond the confines of the small, simple life she'd carved out. There was such hope in her vision that Rue almost cried.

But she saw something else, too. She saw a reserved man struggling and uncomfortable.

"Actually, I came to say something to Rue." Glancing around the table, Andrew looked like he'd rather be anywhere except in Maudie's Diner facing the Tuesday Tarts.

"Andrew," Rue said softly, wishing it was just the two of them but understanding that the women in the room were her loyal friends. "It's okay."

As much as Rue had wanted to believe her date with Andrew had been another encounter with a Bad Man Who Dumped Her, she couldn't help but remember his tenderness, his charm, his sincerity—and the way she'd felt in his arms.

Besides, men and women didn't think alike and they surely didn't act alike. Confronted with a problem, men ran off and did their own thing while women called a committee meeting and got everybody's opinion.

Not that she was letting him off the hook. She still stung from his abrupt departure, but she liked to think of herself as a fair-minded woman who didn't hold grudges. The least she could do was listen to what he had to say, especially since he was making the supreme sacrifice of a reserved man exposing his feelings in public.

"Whatever you want to say, just spit it out, Andrew. I can take it."

"You're making this too easy for me, Rue."

His look of gratitude belied his words. Rue, ever the tender hearted, reached up and touched his hand. The brief touch electrified her.

"It's okay." She spoke to him as if they were the only two people in the room. "Everything's okay. I understand."

"Do you?"

"Yes."

"Then you accept my apology?"

"I accept, Andrew."

To show she was sincere, Rue gave him a genuine smile. In fact, she was relieved.

"Thank you, Rue."

Andrew lingered, as if he had unfinished business with Rue. She couldn't tear her gaze away from his. Holding her breath, she waited. Her friends stopped chattering.

After a small eternity, Andrew left to pick up his take-out order. Something inside Rue folded. What more was there to say? Now she could go back to life as usual.

Sheila and Patsy's daughter, Sophia, sighed audibly, while Patsy beamed.

"See," Sophia said. "My uncle is a good guy."

"You'd get no argument from me," Sheila said. "If I didn't love Rue so much, I'd be wishing I'd kept that date for myself."

Rue was only half listening to the banter swirling around the table. Her mind was on Andrew, probably standing at the cash register paying for the take-out boxes.

When he'd walked out of the room, Rue realized she had more in common with him than she'd first thought. Andrew was as private as she. Like Rue, he apparently didn't like airing his personal affairs in public.

That made his public apology all the more precious to her. Turning back to her friends, she changed the subject to Daisy's baby shower.

Or maybe they were already on the subject. She'd been so wrapped in her feelings for Andrew she wouldn't have known if her hair had caught fire.

CHAPTER NINE

As HE LEFT Maudie's Diner, Andrew felt like a rooster who had cavorted with the head hen and ruffled the feathers of every hen in town. Trying to apologize to Rue in front of witnesses had been the single biggest act of bravery in Andrew's life.

Or so he told himself as he headed to the garage with enough take-out chicken, meat loaf and burgers to feed a third-world country. As his team tore into the boxes, he found himself thinking about Rue.

Ever since she had waltzed in, his life hadn't *felt* normal. He'd wake up in the middle of the night, restless for no reason he could think of. He'd stop in the middle of brushing his teeth, unable to remember if he had already flossed. He'd be scrolling through the TV menu and opt for *An Affair to Remember* over *High Noon*.

Rue had bewitched him.

It was a good thing she'd backed out on Patsy's invitation. He didn't know what would happen if he were cast into her company during the adrenaline high of a NASCAR race.

Andrew's cell phone rang. With a chicken wing in one hand and his cell phone in the other, Andrew thanked his lucky stars the Rue mishap was behind him.

"Andrew Clark," he said into his phone. Now he could get on with his life.

TWO DAYS LATER when Rue opened her shop, she switched on all the lights, put on her hair-cutting apron then put on a CD. When Daisy walked in, she said, "Rue, what is that sappy music?"

"Frank Sinatra."

"He's dead, isn't he? Who in the world listens to him?"

Andrew, Rue almost told her. Instead, she went to the player and put on an album by George Strait. As the country/Western ballad about love lost filled the beauty shop, Rue came to a major decision.

"Daisy, if I go to New York with Patsy, can you handle the shop while I'm gone?"

"Oh, my gosh! You'll get to fly in their private jet. Oh, my goodness!"

"Well? Can you?"

"You bet your sweet patooties I can handle this shop. When's the plane leaving?"

"At noon."

"Then what are you doing standing here?"

Andrew would be at Watkins Glen. As Rue hurried home to pack, she thought about the luxury of having days instead of hours to find out if what she was feeling for Andrew was simply hormones gone wild or if it was something more enduring. True love. The stuff of every woman's dreams.

Including her own. Finally, Rue was ready to admit it.

With her bag in one hand and the morning edition of the paper in the other, Rue climbed into her Mustang. Front page headlines screamed, "Former Champs Vie for 2010 NASCAR Sprint Cup Win." Underneath were photos of Kent Grosso and the good-looking, devil-may-care Garrett in their racing uniforms. One of the patches sewn into the piece that protected the right clavicle of each driver was the same worn by every competitor on the tour, the NASCAR Sprint Cup Series logo. The other simply read Champion.

Rue left her house for the airport an hour early. Though

she knew she'd have time on her hands, she wasn't about to keep Patsy and Dean waiting.

The day was sunny, the weather was still warm, and Rue drove her Mustang with the top down. She even turned on a country/Western station and sang along with every song. Currently, she and Willie Nelson were crooning "Angel Flying Too Close to the Ground."

She didn't know all the words and her singing voice would frighten kids and small dogs, but that didn't bother Rue. She was singing at the top of her lungs.

Life was good. No matter what happened between her and Andrew Clark, Rue intended to enjoy every moment at Watkins Glen.

ANDREW HAD ARRIVED at the hangar early. For one thing, he considered being late a sign of rudeness. Since Garrett and Grace had left yesterday in Andrew's private plane for early sponsor duties, he was his sister and Dean's guest.

For another, he was a stickler for details. Even though Dean and Patsy had a cadre of mechanics to ensure the safety of the plane, Andrew had to see for himself that everything was in working order.

He was doing his second walk-around when he heard the loud music. Some country/Western ballad being sung horribly off-key.

A fairly decent guitar player and a better-than-average harmonica player, Andrew knew his music. He walked onto the tarmac in front of the plane and shielded his eyes.

The music preceded a Mustang. A *familiar* Mustang.

Rue was driving with the top down. Her red hair flew out behind her, bright as the Don Juan roses climbing the arbor in his backyard.

"Reeelease meee," she warbled.

It was all Andrew could do to keep from bursting out

laughing. That was one of his favorite songs, and Rue was slaughtering it.

As she swung into one of the parking slots, he strode toward her Mustang, trying to keep a straight face.

She jumped from her car, a jolt to the senses in tight blue jeans, a bright yellow sweater set and earrings that looked like sunflowers. Or dinner plates. They were so big Andrew could have used them to serve his hot dogs.

When she saw him, Rue's surprise was written all over her face. Obviously she hadn't expected him to be on this plane. In a quick-on-her-feet transformation, she planted her hands on her hips. Her unmistakably defensive gesture amused him.

"What's so funny?" she asked.

"Nothing."

"Then why are you grinning like a jackass eating saw-briars?"

"A jackass?" He'd been called many things, but never that.

For some reason, Andrew found it wildly funny. While he was laughing, Rue stomped around her car and popped her trunk.

"Will you stop that guffawing? If you hadn't noticed, I'm a lady with a big suitcase."

"Allow me."

Andrew hefted her luggage from her trunk. He'd expected something in the nature of a suitcase that would hold enough clothes for an ocean voyage aboard the ill-fated *Titanic*. Instead, Rue had packed in a square case no bigger than one of the larger carry-ons. Burgundy with hot pink polka dots. What else had he expected?

Still, score one for Rue. Most women packed four times what they needed. Then ended up at the stores wherever they traveled buying more.

"Oh, I can't wait to see the inside of this plane." Rue pranced off ahead of him, and Andrew followed.

There was something so lively and carefree about her, he wanted to reach out and touch her. He wanted to see if her joie de vivre would rub off on him.

Was that why he'd been waking, restless, in the middle of the night? The sense that some vital life force was missing from his life?

As always, when he was in cogitation mode, Andrew's long stride slowed to an amble. Over the years, on those rare occasions when loneliness had prompted him to picture himself with a woman, he'd imagined himself falling for someone reserved who would fade into the wallpaper at parties. Somebody like him.

Rue would never fade into the anything, let alone wallpaper.

Andrew made the fatal mistake of glancing ahead to watch her.

Those finely curved hips. The self-confident yet seductive way she walked. The sunshine in her red hair. Her bright circus colors that made you want to turn cartwheels. The heady fragrance of her perfume.

Unexpected desire hit him with the force of a level five hurricane. It was a good thing Patsy and Dean weren't there to see his reaction.

Andrew thanked his lucky stars that he had time to get his inconvenient attraction to Rue out of the way before he had an interested audience. Furthermore, he was glad the object of his desire was in front of him. She probably didn't have a clue about the reaction she was causing.

Suddenly she turned and smiled over her shoulder. Andrew felt like the little boy caught with his hand in the cookie jar. He slowed his steps to put more distance between them.

"Do you mind if I go aboard?"

"Be my guest."

Actually, she was Dean and Patsy's guest, but that was splitting hairs.

Andrew hadn't slowed down with the deliberate intent of watching Rue Larrabee climb a set of stairs, but that was the end result. If he'd thought watching her walk was the biggest test he'd have to his self-control, he'd been horribly mistaken.

Rue on a set of stairs was lethal. Visceral memories assaulted him, and he nearly cracked his teeth biting back a groan.

This was going to be a very long trip.

RUE HOPED Andrew didn't think she was being pushy, racing off to the plane like that, but it was the best she could do under the circumstances. He'd taken her by surprise. She hadn't expected him to be on Patsy and Dean's plane. Besides, the minute she'd laid eyes on Andrew she'd wanted to kiss him.

Kiss him, heck. She'd wanted to throw herself at him like some love-starved spinster.

Okay, she told herself. *Slow down.*

Judging by the way he'd laughed when she got out of the car, he probably already viewed her as somebody so perky she could brew coffee without a pot. She'd just capitalized on that image. Why not? She'd had years of practice being the life of the party.

So what if it kept a safe distance between her and other people. Right now, that's what she needed.

Listen, she wasn't about to repeat the mistake she'd made with Andrew at Cut 'N' Chat. She wanted to take things slow and easy. She wanted to find out what was real and enduring versus what was just need talking.

She stood in the aisle of the posh plane and breathed in the rarified atmosphere of the rich and famous. How easy it would be for Patsy and Dean and Andrew to act snobbish. Fortunately, they acted—and *were*—as ordinary as your next-door neighbor.

Somewhere behind her, Andrew's footsteps echoed on the stairs. Rue put a bright smile on her face and turned to face him.

"I'll just stow your bag," he said.

"Great!" Perky, perky.

She widened her smile as Andrew came toward her. It began to waver when he stopped within touching distance.

"I'll just put it here," he said.

He was so close, she lost all rational thought. She could smell his skin, that wonderful combination of wind and sunshine and all man. She clenched her hands to keep from running them into the V of his open-necked shirt.

"It?"

"Your suitcase."

"Oh."

She couldn't have moved if thirty-five circus elephants and a full brass band were about to mow her down.

Andrew reached over her head, trapping her between his arms. Her hips were pressed against his—*heaven help her*— her nose was at his chin and her eyes were lip level. Delicious lips. Talented lips that had driven her crazy.

Did she make a sound or did he? Laser-blue eyes captured hers. Suddenly the two of them were suspended in a cocoon of heat and desire, flame and temptation. Like a romantic movie classic in slow motion, his lips descended toward hers.

Rue held her breath. He was going to kiss her. And she would be putty, helpless in his arms, unable to stop herself from kissing him back.

His breath was warm against her face, his lips only a hair's breadth away. And Rue was drowning. If she went under this time, she'd never regain her feet. She'd never be able to spend the next few days calmly assessing the situation, trying to decide if opposites did attract or if she and Andrew were destined to be a one-night stand.

It took every reserve of willpower Rue possessed to duck under his arm and out of his reach.

"This is fabulous! It'll be like flying in the comfort of your own living room." She tried for perky, and failed miserably.

To his credit, Andrew had to visibly collect himself before he could answer.

"Patsy and Dean go first class." He managed to sound nonchalant. Briefly. "They even have champagne."

Fraught with layers of meaning, the word hung between them a full five seconds. On the heels of the almost-kiss, Rue came undone.

She could hear the rush of her blood. The throb of her pulse felt like a drumbeat. *Take me, take me, take me.*

Oh, help.

"Rue…"

"Don't say anything." She held up her hand. "Not one word, Andrew." He opened his mouth and she practically shouted. "Not a word. I am not a ripe plum for just any old body to come along and pick."

Racing toward the back of the plane she burst through the door to the bathroom and leaned her head against the cool tiles.

So much for perky. That act had lasted all of five minutes.

What other barriers would fall before this trip was over?

CHAPTER TEN

A RIPE PLUM FOR just any old body to come along and pick?

Her statement said volumes about Rue's character. All of it good. He would have laughed out loud if Rue hadn't been so visibly upset. Though why he felt such relief, he couldn't say.

Or wouldn't say. With the challenge of Watkins Glen still ahead, Andrew couldn't afford to let Rue make him lose focus.

What was taking her so long? He marched down the aisle and tapped on the bathroom door.

"Rue?"

"What!"

She was prickly. Andrew was relieved to add a negative to his growing catalog of Rue's traits. As a man who always controlled his temper, he couldn't imagine himself with a woman who let every feeling show.

"I just wondered if you're all right."

"Of course, I'm *all right*. Andrew Clark, if you think I'm going to let you mess up my good time, you've got another *think* coming."

"Well...I didn't say that."

"No man messes up my good time."

Where was all that passion coming from? Was it possible Rue had been hurt by men in the same way he'd been hurt by women. If he paid attention to such things, he'd know, but Andrew was not one to listen to local gossip.

"Did you hear me, Andrew?"

"Yes, ma'am."

"I heard that grin. Are you taking me lightly?"

"I wouldn't think of it."

"Good. Don't… And another thing. I didn't come on this trip just to be near you."

"I didn't say you did."

"And there will be no repeats of our frolic at Cut 'N' Chat."

"Frolic?"

"That's what I said."

His grin broadened. "Why don't you open the door and come out so we can talk about that?"

Rue was quiet so long he almost put his ear to the door to find out what she was doing in there. He could feel sweat collecting in the edge of his hair while he waited. Doggone that woman. She heated him up in more ways than he wanted to think about.

Finally the door eased open a bit and Rue stuck her head around the crack.

"I don't want to talk about it."

"Okay. We'll talk about baseball."

"Baseball?"

"Yeah. Do you like the St. Louis Cardinals?"

"I think they walk on water."

Andrew didn't even let himself chalk up her love of his favorite team. He told himself it didn't matter. He was simply passing the time till Dean and Patsy arrived.

Grinning, Rue sashayed out, plopped into a seat, crossed her legs and started swinging her right foot. Her booted foot.

Rue was wearing red cowgirl boots. What else?

Andrew didn't make the mistake of grinning again. Rue had more prickles than a desert cactus. He wasn't about to grin himself into another corner where he'd have to talk his way out.

Fortunately, he didn't have to do anything. When Patsy and Dean bustled in, their excitement and big personalities electrified the plane's cabin.

Andrew sat back, buckled in and breathed a sigh of relief. The only problem was, his gaze kept straying toward Rue. As the plane taxied down the runway and charted a course north, the thing he concentrated most on was trying to forget how her kisses tasted and how she had felt in his arms.

THE WEATHER WAS BEAUTIFUL for flying. Dean's pilot set the plane down in record time.

When Andrew emerged, his spirits lifted at the sight of the FastMax plane parked near the hangar, along with about thirty other private jets. Separating himself from Patsy and her guest, he whipped out his cell phone to call his stepson.

"Garrett, how does everything look?"

"The car's here, looking good, and the weather prediction for the weekend is hundred percent sunshine. It'll be a hot track."

Speaking of hot, Rue was off the plane. Andrew could smell her perfume. He made himself concentrate on matters at hand.

"Better than a wet one," he told Garrett, and then had an erotic image that wouldn't go away. "I'll be there in twenty minutes."

"The roads are already jam packed. It'll probably take you an hour or longer."

That was fine with Andrew. An hour would give him time to get himself under control.

The rental cars were already waiting, one for Andrew, the other for Dean, Patsy and Rue. His sister's efficiency at work.

But leave it to her to pick sports models. Two convertibles just begging for the tops to go down.

"Great." Rue was as excited as a kid at a Christmas shop.

Dragging his attention away from Rue, Andrew pocketed his phone and walked over to kiss his sister on the cheek. "'Bye, Patsy. See you later."

"At dinner tonight, Andrew. Don't you dare miss it."

"I'll try my best to be there." Andrew put on his sunglasses and grabbed his bag. "But I make no promises."

Since it would be impolite not to say anything at all to Rue, Andrew turned and waved in her general direction to indicate his goodbye included everybody.

When he strode off he was whistling. It wasn't until he'd gotten into his car that he realized it was the Ray Charles song Rue had been singing. "Release Me." A song about love gone wrong.

The only good thing Andrew could say about his song choice was that the bottom line was appropriate.

Andrew was at a crossroads. If he wanted any peace of mind, he had to make another choice: free himself of his improbable attraction to Rue or follow it and see where it led.

AFTER THEY'D CHECKED IN, Rue had the rest of the afternoon to herself. Andrew was at the track and Patsy and Dean were immediately caught up in television and newspaper interviews as well as meetings with sponsors.

Rue took a leisurely swim in the pool, then put on shorts and a T-shirt and went for a stroll around the hotel grounds.

The sun was already going down when she stepped back into the lobby. And there was Andrew, caught in the beam of camera lights and fielding questions from a cadre of reporters. Seeing him so unexpectedly tripped her heart into double time. She'd thought he'd still be at the track.

Rue stood just on the periphery of the lights, along with

hundreds of other race fans eager for autographs and firsthand information.

"Mr. Clark, do you expect FastMax to win back-to-back Sprint Cups?"

Andrew's smile was easy, his stance exuded confidence. "I always expect to win."

"Last year Garrett was the underdog. What would you call him now?"

"Racing is a team effort. Always. I'd call FastMax the team everybody has to beat."

Rue shivered. This was an Andrew she'd never seen up close and personal, a self-assured, strongly competitive businessman. She'd known she was traveling with the powerhouses of NASCAR racing, but seeing Andrew in action gave her a visceral satisfaction she knew would keep her awake long into the night.

Fascinated, she found herself caught in the beams of his blue eyes. Was his sudden boyish smile just for her? Rue wrapped her arms around herself, shivering. When Andrew was whisked off toward the meeting rooms, probably to meet with sponsors, Rue went back outside to walk along the water's edge. She needed to collect herself before dinner.

AS FAR AS RUE was concerned, the restaurant on Seneca Lake was perfect—soul-satisfying food, down-home atmosphere and cheerful waitstaff. Patsy and Dean had gotten a choice table overlooking the water.

Rue had ordered corn-and-lobster chowder which was so delicious it should come with a warning that it was possibly addictive. But as much as she relished the food, the best part of the meal was sitting beside Andrew. In the presence of Patsy and Dean, Grace and Garrett, Sophia and her husband, Justin Murphy, and Kent and his wife, Tanya, Andrew's personality shone through.

And Rue liked what she saw, a man who loved his family and laughed often. Without the pressure of being on a date with him, Rue fell into the comfort of easy camaraderie.

She could get used to this.

"I'm sorry to leave early, but I need to get to the track." Andrew pushed back his chair.

"Why don't you take Rue so she can see the track at night?" Patsy said.

"Rue?" Andrew surprised her by asking.

"I'd love to."

Her answer pleased Patsy, but it wasn't her friend Rue intended to please. For once, when something good was offered, she wasn't going to rationalize and trump up reasons why she shouldn't seize the moment. She was going to follow her heart.

He took her arm and escorted her from the restaurant. A gentlemanly gesture that felt intensely personal. Shivers rolled over her, partly from the breeze coming off the water, but mostly from sheer excitement.

Without a word, Andrew pulled off his jacket and draped it over her shoulders, his hands lingering.

"That feels good, Andrew."

"You're wearing such a light wrap I thought you might need my coat."

Maybe it was the moonlight. Maybe it was the moment. Whatever the reason, Rue felt daring.

"I'm talking about your hands."

Andrew trailed his fingers lightly across her cheek, then opened the car door and she slid into the passenger seat.

"I've never ridden with you in a convertible." She was glad the moonlight covered her flush.

"We'll have to remedy that. Do you mind if we drive with the top down?"

"Not at all. I love the night sky."

"So do I."

He drove the way he did everything else, with expert ease. Totally comfortable, Rue leaned her head back. The sky almost took her breath away—a crescent moon and a billion stars flung across a deep blue velvet canvas.

"Pinch me if I'm dreaming," she murmured, and that said it all.

ANDREW COULD HARDLY keep his eyes on the road for watching Rue. Without artifice, she had totally abandoned herself to the enjoyment of the drive. It thrilled him that she enjoyed simple pleasures—a quiet dinner with his family, the wind in her hair, the constellations, a long drive without the need to clutter it with chatter.

She was still quiet when he took her hand and led her into the empty stands of the race track. Though there were signs of the pending race all around them—the closed-up haulers, the motor homes, spurts of activity near the track—without the frantic scene of racing cars and pit crews and a hundred thousand screaming fans, the track looked serene, almost surreal.

Beside him, Rue became very still. Andrew started to ask her what she thought, but at his second instinct made him look at her instead. Tears glistened on her cheeks.

"Rue?"

"Do you feel it, Andrew?"

He did, of course, but he was quiet, waiting for her to put her feelings into words.

"Everything is right here," she said. "The energy, the excitement, the spirit of millions of drivers and families and fans who love NASCAR racing." She smiled at him. "Thank you."

For the second time since he'd met Rue, Andrew saw her as a woman he might love.

He traced the tears on her cheeks, then moved his fingers across her lips. Her breath hitched, but she stood on the bleachers, waiting for what he would do next.

Andrew didn't ponder his next move. It was as natural as breathing. He kissed her. She tasted of sweet creamery butter and mulled cider, of passion and promise, of moonlight and magic.

The kiss had its own momentum, and Andrew found himself hauling Rue against his body, urging her closer as she gave in to her feelings.

If it was possible to feel passion in every bone and sinew, now was the moment.

If there had been a bed nearby, a sofa or even four walls and a floor, Andrew would have seized the moment. But this was not the place, not the time. Too much was at stake to get sidetracked by passion.

But once he'd shifted gears and floored the gas, it wasn't that easy to bring his runaway desire to a standstill.

He eased his hold, trying to catch a deep breath and regain control.

"Andrew." Rue leaned back. "I don't want to rush into things again."

If she hadn't wanted it, she had certainly put on a good show. Andrew's first reaction was to say, *you're right* and walk away. His better nature told him to hold still.

In one of life's great twists of irony, Andrew discovered that the Man Who Doesn't Understand Woman longed for the woman he'd thought totally unsuitable. He longed for her, not merely as the current object of his desire, but as a woman who would bring a new dimension into his life, a sense of fun and laughter and joy he hadn't even known he was missing until he'd met Rue Larrabee.

But was he willing to go the next step and risk his sorry history repeating itself?

"What do you want, Rue?"

"Not you. Not like this."

"You could have fooled me."

"Oh, dear." She stepped back and ran her hands through her hair. "I said that wrong. I didn't mean, not you, specifically."

"It sounded pretty specific."

"Actually, I do want you. Probably more than I've ever wanted any man. But not here. Not like this."

"You're right. Though I imagine this track has seen all kinds of thrills, I don't want to add to the lore."

Rue smiled, and he took it as a good sign.

"It seems we're explosive together, Andrew."

"Yes. We keep proving that."

"I don't want to let passion get in the way of getting to know who you really are."

"What you see is the real me. I don't play games, Rue."

"I have to be certain. I can't let you be just another man who breaks my heart."

Andrew didn't want to break her heart. But did he want to keep it? It was time to put on the brakes and decide exactly what he wanted to do with this complex woman who could entice him, madden him and enchant him, all within the space of five minutes.

"I'll take you back to the Harbor Inn."

"I know you have work to do here. I can hang around until you're finished."

"I could be here all night." He picked up her sweater and his jacket, then draped both of them over her shoulders. "Besides, you've already proved to be a bigger distraction than I can handle."

"Would you call that a good start on getting to know you?"

"Rue, I think we got to know each other at Cut 'N' Chat."

"Don't remind me. I'm trying to reform."

Twenty minutes later they arrived at the hotel. "Promise me one thing."

"What?"

"You won't change too much. I kinda like you the way you are."

"I noticed."

"Good."

Andrew left her at her door, but he didn't kiss her. He didn't dare. Not with her bed just a couple of feet away.

CHAPTER ELEVEN

FOR RUE, THE next few days were jammed with every kind of excitement imaginable. With Max, Patsy and Dean's driver at her disposal, as well as a rental car, she was free to go anywhere she wanted. They, as well as Andrew, were constantly besieged by the press and their obligations to sponsors.

Though Watkins Glen was a great spot for tourists, Rue hadn't come to sightsee. She spent most of her time at the track. The day of the practice runs, Grace invited her for breakfast in the motor home she and Garrett shared in the Drivers' and Owners' Lot, accessible only through a security gate.

With homemade biscuits, sausage, bacon, Nassau grits and tomato gravy, breakfast was a gourmet feast. Not surprising considering Grace's cooking talents.

The big surprise was Andrew. Just as Grace was pouring coffee, he came through the door.

"Coffee smells good, Grace." He clasped his son's shoulder, kissed his daughter-in-law's cheek, then leaned down and brushed his lips across Rue's. She thought she'd die of happiness on the spot.

"Sit down," Grace told him. "You need to eat."

"No time. I'm having breakfast with the sponsors. Can you fix me coffee to go?"

"You bet."

His gaze captured Rue for a heady second, then he turned

to Garrett and said, "Good luck, son. You're a champ and don't you forget it."

"Thanks, Dad."

"Rue." He leaned in close and handed her a FastMax T-shirt and cap. "Will you wear these? For me?"

"Oh, my goodness. Yes!"

"If you'll promise to cheer loudly, Garrett might sign them." Andrew gave her a wink and another quick kiss, and before she could react, he grabbed his coffee and was out the door.

"Looks like you and Dad have a thing going."

"Hush up, Garrett. You're embarrassing her." Grace kissed him. "For luck, baby. Now get your cute butt out of here and drive like a champ."

Garrett posted great laps in each of the two morning practices while Rue sat beside Grace in her newly signed FastMax finery and cheered.

LATE THAT NIGHT, Rue was so wound up she could hardly sleep. Between the excitement of seeing her first out of town NASCAR race and thinking about Andrew's quick kisses in front of his family, Rue had rolled her sheet into knots.

Switching on the light, she padded to the bathroom, then glanced at the clock. Major mistake. It was 2:00 a.m. and she knew she'd never fall asleep in her current state.

Throwing on sweats and jogging shoes, she stuffed her cell phone and her room key into her pocket and eased out the door. It was another gorgeous, moonlit night. Maybe a stroll around the hotel grounds would clear her head.

Most women would have been afraid to be alone, but not Rue. As owner of her own business, she'd seen and handled everything. Besides, the hotel was crawling with NASCAR fans and family. She'd be as safe as if she were in her own front yard.

Still, she stayed within the perimeters of the parking lot

lights. That light plus the moonlight assured that Rue wouldn't step off into a pothole and break her neck.

As she rounded the east side of the hotel, she heard the haunting, visceral strains of a harmonica. A favored instrument of both blues and country/Western artists, a harmonica in the hands of a skilled musician could break your heart, then pick up the pieces, patch them back together and hand the renewed heart to you on a silver platter.

Feeling as if every blood vessel she had was just beneath her skin, Rue stood still, listening. The song was "Moon River," a ballad about love lost but never forgotten.

Following the music, Rue rounded the corner of the hotel and saw a shadow underneath an outside stairwell. The shadow must have seen her, too, because the music faded into the night.

"Don't stop. It's beautiful."

"Rue?"

"Andrew? You're a musician, too?"

"I wouldn't call it that. I like to fool around with my harmonica and guitar, that's all."

For some foolish reason, Rue felt as if she'd been handed the award for being steadfast and good. She'd heard Patsy say that Andrew preferred hotels to a motor home at the track, but she'd never imagined an accidental encounter with him in the moonlight.

"Do you mind if I listen? I *adore* the sound of a harmonica."

"I don't play for just anybody."

"I'm not just anybody."

Silence. Rue could hear her own heartbeat, feel every inch of her skin, but she still saw Andrew as only a shadow.

"No, Rue, you're not."

As she walked toward him, cooled by the night air and heated by anticipation, Andrew moved from underneath the stairwell and put his harmonica to his lips. The deep mysteries of night transformed him to a man of moonlight, music and magic.

Rue felt as if she'd landed in the middle of her own classic movie. With the faded strains of "Moon River" still echoing, she could be Audrey Hepburn about to discover love in *Breakfast at Tiffany's.* A heady, delicious prospect. And a bit frightening.

She sank onto the stairs, the concrete step cool underneath her sweats, her long legs stretched out in front of her.

She glanced up at Andrew and smiled. He put his harmonica to his lips, cupped his hands around the small silver instrument to create perfect resonance and began to play. Throwing himself heart, soul and body into his harmonica, Andrew made love to her with music.

It was both erotic and tender, and she fell hopelessly, madly, irrevocably in love.

As the stars began to fade and the moon's path across the water became faint and silvery, Andrew pocketed his harmonica then offered his arm and escorted her back to her room.

"Thank you for a perfect evening, Andrew."

"Thank *you,* Rue. You're a kind, generous-hearted woman."

"I try to be, but I'm not your ideal woman, Andrew. I don't even come close."

"Rue, I need to say this. When I left you that morning, I'd had a phone call from a former pit boss. I didn't want to disturb you and I didn't want to stay too long and put you in a compromising position."

She put her hand on his lips. "It's okay. It's over and done with. Forgotten."

"I'm not good with women. You might say I'm terrible with them."

"If anybody else said that about you, I'd slap them silly."

His chuckle started deep in his chest before it exploded to full-blown laughter.

"Rue, I can laugh more easily with you than any woman I've ever known."

"Is that a good thing?"

"It's a good thing." He cupped her face and tipped it up to his. "A *very* good thing."

He kissed her then, a soft, tender kiss with lips still warm and puffy from his silver harmonica. The kiss was brief but filled with promise, a perfect ending to the single most magical evening Rue had ever known.

She went into her room, fell onto her bed and touched her lips. *There. Where his had been.*

If she never had another moment with him, if tomorrow Andrew walked out of her life and never came back, she would have this evening.

"WELCOME TO THE RACES!"

The announcement was followed by an opening prayer and a rousing rendition of "The Star-Spangled Banner." The fans rose to their feet as the song was punctuated by the sound and spectacle of two jets flying overhead and exploding oil cans—"bombs bursting in air."

It was a gorgeous Sunday afternoon with a maximum capacity crowd there to cheer on their favorite NASCAR drivers.

Though Rue loved Bart Branch, Kent Grosso, Justin Murphy and all the drivers she considered *hers,* she—along with thousands of other fans—was cheering for Garrett Clark.

"Gentlemen, start your engines!"

The roar from forty-three engines and more wildly cheering fans split the air as the drivers, all skilled and daring men, blazed around the track.

Rue jumped up and down and pumped her fist. "Go Garrett."

For the first fifteen laps, Kent Grosso dominated the track, with Bart holding on to a narrow second in a heart-thundering, edge-of-the-seat competition. But Garrett was moving up fast.

"That'a boy, Garrett," Rue said. "Come on, come on."

Suddenly the car in front of Andrew's stepson spun out. Rue made a sound of dismay and Patsy squeezed her hand.

The crowd went into a screaming frenzy. Time seemed to move in slow motion as cars going at speeds of one hundred and thirty miles an hour corrected to avoid collision.

Rue found herself saying one word, over and over—*please*. It was half plea, half prayer. She wouldn't even let herself think beyond the moment.

When the spinning car came to a halt off the track and the other cars roared safely past, Rue let go of Patsy's hand and slumped into her seat. Events that had actually taken only seconds seemed like hours, and she was drained.

Rue searched for sight of Andrew without success. She had not seen him since he'd left her at her door last night. He'd probably left mere hours after that for the track. She wondered if he'd even slept.

But most of all, she wondered if he'd felt even half of what she had there in that secluded spot near the stairwell. After the excitement and glamour of the weekend faded, after Andrew returned to FastMax and she returned to Cut 'N' Chat, would he still make love to her with music? Would she still feel breathless at the mere sight of him?

Below her, Bart Branch's car pulled in for a pit stop. Though his crew had him back on the track in eleven seconds, that's all it took for Garrett to smoke into first place.

Garrett, in the No. 402 car, dominated the race for three more laps, but Victory Lane was not in the cards for Andrew's stepson—nor for Kent Grosso. Jeb Stallworth was the winner. Still, Rue was on such a NASCAR high she thought she might float through the rest of the night.

THAT EVENING, Dr. and Mrs. Joel Gladney, longtime NASCAR fans and friends of Dean and Patsy, hosted a huge party at their posh home on Seneca Lake. Though everybody usually left right after the races, Patsy had talked her family into staying for the party. The huge white tent, erected on the lawn beside the lake, was teeming with guests.

Over the rim of her champagne glass, Rue watched as Patsy, Dean, Kent, Andrew and Garrett greeted fans and well-wishers.

With his arm draped around his stepson's shoulders, Andrew looked totally at ease. Occasionally he lifted his head to scan the crowd, but Rue lingered near the edges. She wasn't about to steal Andrew away from his evening with his family.

Rue slipped from the tent and followed the boardwalk along the edges of the water. A light breeze stirred the hem of her green chiffon skirt, and she drew her velvet shawl closer around her shoulders. In the distance she spotted a gazebo.

Enchanted, Rue followed the boardwalk till she came to the steps leading down. The gazebo was right over the water and gave her the feeling that she might be dreaming.

Rue leaned her elbows on the railing and watched the play of moonlight over the water. Behind her, the party tent was a smear of white, the party noise a mere echo.

"You look peaceful."

Andrew. Shivers ran through Rue as he leaned against the railing, so close she could feel his body heat.

"I didn't hear you coming."

"So I noticed."

"You shouldn't be here. You should be with Garrett."

"I wanted to see you."

"Why?"

He wrapped his arms around her and drew her close. "For this." He kissed her earlobe, her eyes, her cheeks. "And this."

This was no small, chaste, good-night kiss at the door of her hotel room. This was a mind-bending, heart-thumping kiss that left no doubt whatsoever that Andrew wanted her.

In the gazebo, with the moonlight over the deep waters of the lake, Rue felt like a Southern belle in a historical romance novel.

"We seem to do this at the most inconvenient times," Andrew said.

"But in the most spectacular places." Rue sighed. "I always dreamed of building a gazebo like this in my backyard."

"Don't change the subject."

"What subject?"

"Us."

"Is there an *us,* Andrew?"

He kissed her again, a deep, soul-satisfying kiss that left her weak-kneed and wanting more.

"Isn't it obvious?" he whispered.

"Yes." But was love this easy? Her history didn't bear that out. "And no."

"Don't start playing games with me now, Rue. Not after we've come this far."

"I'm not playing games. I just have to be certain that this is real and we're not simply caught up in the excitement of the weekend."

"Is that what you really think, Rue? That this is just a carry-over thrill from the track?"

"I don't know what to think anymore. I need time to figure it out."

Andrew cupped her face and looked deeply into her eyes.

Was he going to kiss her again? Whisk her off to the Harbor Inn and make love to her? Tell her he loved her, loved *her,* for goodness sake, not some fanciful idea of who Rue Larrabee might be.

When he finally let go, Rue's heart fell. Maybe that was her answer.

"We should get back to the party," he said.

Rue nodded. Conversation was no longer an option for her. If she opened her mouth she might say *I love you,* and she wouldn't do that. He had to say it first.

ANDREW WENT HOME in the FastMax jet. Altogether it was best. He needed to spend more time with Garrett, analyzing the race at Watkins Glen and strategizing for the next one at Michigan, and he wanted to give Rue—and himself—some breathing room.

Though he believed his feelings were true, he believed he'd found a woman he could spend the rest of his life loving, he needed to see if there was a ring of truth in what Rue had said. Would their feelings hold up once they returned to life in Mooresville?

She'd asked for time and he'd give it to her. Besides, Rue was worth the wait.

THOUGH RUE GOT HOME early Monday afternoon, she didn't go back into her shop till Tuesday. Every time the phone rang, she expected it to be Andrew. By Tuesday night, she'd exhausted herself with anticipation.

She thought of opting out of the Tuesday Tarts meeting, but she didn't want to raise suspicions and eyebrows. Fortunately, all the talk was of next week's race at Michigan.

When she went to bed Tuesday evening, there had still been no word from Andrew. Not even a phone call, let alone a personal appearance. Apparently Rue had been right. Although her feelings were holding up fine, his had apparently taken a nosedive. It appeared loving Andrew Clark was going to be another long, lonely, one-way street.

When Rue woke up on Wednesday, she was in a snit. It didn't help that somebody was hammering outside. The racket was so loud it sounded like it was right beneath her window.

In her bare feet and a nightshirt that said, Who Died and Made You Queen?, Rue raced downstairs, through her kitchen and out the back door. Her yard was piled with lumber and sawhorses and skill saws. And in the midst of it all was a lone purple phalaenopsis orchid…and Andrew, wielding a hammer.

"Good morning," he said.

"Good grief!"

"Is that all you have to say?" Andrew laid down his hammer and scooped her close.

"What do you want me to say?"

"Yes."

"What's the question?"

"Will you marry me?"

"Give me one good reason why I should."

"I'll give you three. I'm building you a gazebo."

"That's only one."

"How about, I love you?"

"Are you sure?"

"Never more sure in my life, Rue. Do you love me?"

"I fell for you the minute you walked into my shop and perched your big, sexy self on that little bitty chair. Still, that's only two."

"I know." Andrew kissed her and they didn't come up for a long, long time. "Which way is the bedroom?"

"Why?"

"I'm going to show you reason number three."

And for a very long time, he did.

The woman who had spent her life rescuing others was now being rescued. And it was the grandest rescue of all. Andrew Clark was saving the heart of Rue Larrabee. Even better, she was saving his right back.

* * * * *